SHORT & TALL TALES
IN
GOOSE PIMPLE
JUNCTION

Short & Tall Tales
in
Goose Pimple
Junction

by

Amy Metz

Southern
Ink
Press

Copyright © 2015 Amy Metz

Published by Southern Ink Press
1st Edition
Volume 3 of the Goose Pimple Junction mystery series

Cover by Anne Rackley www.annerackley.com

Cover design and Interior design and formatting by:

E.M.
TIPPETTS
BOOK DESIGNS

www.emtippettsbookdesigns.com

Printed in the United States of America

SUMMARY: This is not your average Southern town. With a hint of mystery, a lot of laughs, and its unique charm, you'll catch a glimpse of everyday life in Goose Pimple Junction in this short story compilation. *Short & Tall Tales* occurs chronologically between *Murder & Mayhem*, book 1, and *Heroes & Hooligans*, book 2, in the Goose Pimple Junction mystery series. *Tales* is a fun escape that will answer questions readers may have about the residents of this quirky small town.

ISBN: 978-0-9897140-6-8

TABLE OF CONTENTS

SHORT TALES

TALL TALE: ONE BAD APPLE

REC IPES

Dedicated to
The folks of Stockbridge, Massachusetts – my Northern Goose Pimple Junction

SHORT TALES

A Right Good Choice

Some people don't have any walking-around sense.

~Southern certitude

"There goes Pete the Greek with *that woman*." Estherlene Baumgarten glared out the diner's big picture window that looked onto Main Street in downtown Goose Pimple Junction. "Look how she's dressed. Putting on airs and all."

"He's been seeing her for some time now, don't you know?" Junebug fixed the pins that held a bun to the top of her head as her eyes followed the couple walking down the street.

"Doesn't he know she and Homer Wensley ate supper without saying grace?"

"Well, not only him . . . " Junebug had heard Tallulah's morals were questionable, but she was trying to be delicate. "Once she had Homer's kid, he moved on, and . . . " Junebug raised an eyebrow, "she moved on and on and on."

Clive and Earl came into the diner, in the midst of another one of their *lively discussions*, and took their regular seats at the bar. The two older men had whiled away many hours arguing over anything and everything on those red vinyl stools, but when all was said and done, either one of them would take a bullet for the other – and most of the residents of Goose Pimple Junction as well.

"Did not." Earl slapped his hand on the counter.

"She absogaldernlutely *did*." Clive turned to Junebug as if to signal the discussion closed, but Earl wasn't quite ready.

"Junie, old Clive here expects me to believe Carla Sue — may she rest in peace — once found Tallulah Bogarde and Patrick Dobbins in . . . uh . . . in flagrante delicto."

"In fragrant what?" Junebug put her hands on her hips, her brow furrowed.

"Not fragrant." Earl rolled his eyes and let out an impatient sigh. "You know…in *amorous congress.*"

Junebug stared at him with narrowed eyes and a confused look on her face. She looked at Estherlene. "You know what this fool is talking about?"

"Junebug," Estherlene said as if she were talking to a child, "rumor has it she *found* them." She waggled her head. "You know. Bread-and-butter fashion."

"Oh. Why didn't you say so in the first place? Sure she did. I was just telling Estherlene here that woman has sweet-talked — and Lord knows what else — just about any man on two legs." She looked through the open window into the kitchen at her husband, Slick. "Except for Slick. He knows I won't tolerate none of those shenanigans."

"You're all the woman I need, Junebug," Slick called through the window. "You're the cheese to my macaroni."

"And you're the milk to my cookie. Now get back to work. Table three's waiting, sugar." Her voice sounded harsh, but the smile and look that Junebug gave to her husband said that it was merely banter. The two were clearly crazy about each other.

Clive seemed amused. "Is that how Patrick got his nickname?"

Just then, Louetta Stafford and Tess Tremaine walked in. "What nickname? Who y'all gossiping about?" Louetta asked. She looked resplendent in a hot pink polka dot dress.

"Moon Dobbins," Junebug said, pouring coffee into a cup.

"I call people by their given name. I don't stand for all that foolishness," Earl mumbled.

"Everybody calls Patrick 'Moon,'" Louetta said, sliding her ample bottom onto a counter stool. "Didn't you know that? I thought everybody knew that. Is *what* how he got his nickname?"

Tess slid onto a stool next to Louetta. "I don't believe I know Mr. Dobbins, do I?"

Estherlene, who was known for her big mouth and extensive knowledge of the goings-on in the community, answered her. "His wife found Tallulah and Moon in *convivial society.*"

"And y'all think that's how he got his nickname? I always thought it was on account of the cheeks on his *face.*" Junebug put a cup of coffee in front of Clive and Earl.

"Junebug!" Tess clamped her hand over her mouth.

"Now, Junie, don't be ugly," Clive cautioned. "Gimmee a piece of that buttermilk pie, will ya, darlin'?"

"Sure." She nodded in Earl's direction. "Whatta you want, Earl?"

"I'll make it easy on you. Make it the same."

"You always do everything I do." Clive slapped his hand down on the counter. "Why don't you grow a brain and think for yourself?"

"Then what would I need you for?" Earl winked at Junebug, and she went off to get their order.

Estherlene spoke up, addressing Louetta and Tess. "You know she's carrying on with Pete the Greek now, don't cha? That's what got us started on the subject. We seen them walking up yonder."

"I don't see anything wrong with it," Clive grumped. "As my mother would say, we none have the promise of tomorrow, so enjoy today. Can't fault old Pete for doing that. He's a widower, you know."

Junebug came back with the pie. "My mama used to say a reputation is better 'n great wealth."

"That's Proverbs," Estherlene corrected.

"Nuh uh," Clive said. "It's Ecclesiastes."

"It's both, y'all. To one degree or another." Louetta asked for sweet tea and then said, "'Course it would be nice to have both."

"Huh?" Clive said.

Louetta took the glass of tea from Junebug. "A good reputation and great wealth. Keep up, will ya?"

"Of course there was Claude Tally too," Estherlene said.

"What about Claude Tally?" Earl asked.

"I heard he had a *brush* with Tallulah once." Clive waggled his eyebrows.

"If there's one rat you can see, there's gonna be fifty you can't." Junebug refilled everyone's cup of coffee. As she set the pot back down on its burner, she turned to look out the diner's plate glass window. "Now there's a peculiar one." She nodded her head toward the street. "Honey Winchester. She never met a man she didn't like, if you know what I mean. Why, she'd steal one right out from under the best of us if given half a chance. She's got the morals of an alley cat."

"Well, now that we've slandered half of Goose Pimple, who's gonna talk to Pete the Greek?" Clive asked.

"Will you just call the man Pete?" Earl mumbled.

"Why do y'all call him Pete the Greek?" Tess looked from face to face. Everyone stared at her like she had two heads, but Louetta spoke up.

"First of all, I'm right proud of you, Tessie. You're talking more like a southerner everyday. Secondly, we call him Pete the Greek because he's from Greece, darlin'."

"Why's anybody gotta talk to him? It's his private bidness." Earl shook his head in disgust.

"But he's new in town," Clive said. "He retired down here from upstate who-knows-where. He might not know about her checkered past. And what if he finds out about it when it's too late? I think somebody oughtta tell him."

"You shouldenoughtta get involved." Earl jabbed his finger at his friend.

Clive jabbed his finger back at Earl. "The man's got a right to know he's carrying on with a loose woman."

THE OPPORTUNITY to talk to Pete presented itself a few weeks later, right after his and Tallulah's engagement was announced. Pete came into the diner and sat down next to Earl and Clive. Earl, knowing what Clive intended to do and wanting no part of it, politely excused himself, threw some bills on the counter, and left the diner.

"That Earl." Clive slowly shook his head. "I've known him since dirt was new. He's good people, but a little high-strung, ya know?"

"I expect he is," Pete the Greek said in his thick accent.

"Hireyew doing, Pete?"

"Clive, if I was doing any better, I'd be twins."

Junebug arrived and Pete ordered coffee and a burger. Before she went to put in the order, she said, "I hear congratulations are in order. You gonna go and getcherself hitched?"

"Looks a like, Ms. Junebug. I got a tired of waiting on Slick to keel over, so what choice did I a have?" He gestured to Slick with a big smile on his face.

Clive's ears perked up at the unknowing lead-in Pete had just given him. "Seems like a fine man of your caliber has a lot of choices."

"I think, as the locals around here say, I've made a right good choice."

"Well now, how long have you been on the market, Pete? Didn't your wife pass not too long ago? What's the rush?"

"No rush. I just found a da woman I want to spend a da rest of my life with, and dat's what we're a gonna to do."

"How much do you really know about Tallulah?"

Junebug set down Pete's burger and coffee in front of him and gave a pointed look to Clive before she retreated to tend to a table in the back.

"I know all I need to know, Clive." Pete put ketchup on the hamburger.

"Are you sure? You know, some women tell enough lies to ice a wedding cake."

Pickle came through the door, wearing a T-shirt that said: I SPILL THINGS. And sure enough, there was a big red stain on the left side of his shirt.

"How do, Pickle? You come in to get some more food on your shirt?"

Pickle stopped next to Clive, looking confused. "Uh . . . no, sir. I came in to meet Charlotte."

Clive clapped him on the back. "Well then, get on, son." He turned back to Pete and hitched his thumb at Pickle's retreating back. "That kid's got clue deficit disorder." Then in a nonchalant way that was so nonchalant it was obvious, he said, "You know anyone like that?"

Pete looked him in the eye and smiled. "I suppose I do, Clive."

Clive worked on Pete for a little longer, getting nowhere. Pete was either too dense or too stubborn. Clive decided it was time to be blunt.

"Pete, I like you."

"I lika you too, Clive."

"And I want what's best for you."

"Thank you." He took a bite and looked at Clive warily over the burger.

"But I don't think Tallulah is it."

"Is what?"

Finally, Clive flatly said, "Pete, you have to know that she's slept with half of the men in Goose Pimple Junction!"

Pete was silent for a moment, showing no emotion on his face. He took another bite of his hamburger, chewed, and swallowed. Then he replied, "Goose Pimple Junction, she no big a da town."

Is it Hot Enough For You?

A good attitude spreads like kudzu.

~Southern belief

Lard was Slick's secret ingredient. Nobody knew what made his food taste so good (so good that your feet couldn't stay still) except for Slick and his wife, Junebug. His supply was getting low, so he headed over to Fern & Moody's General Store. Moody Phillips had a few pigs on his farm and was Slick's only source for lard. The store was known for its specialty items, but to Slick the most special item was the lard. As he walked to the store, he took his comb from his pocket and slicked back his hair. Guess how he got his nickname?

Mayor Buck came out of the Muffin Man wiping his brow. "How do, Slick. Is it hot enough for you?"

Slick nodded. "Yep." He was a man of few words.

"I tell you what, I'm about to roast. I'm gonna go on down to the office and not come out until the sun goes down. You take care now." Buck clapped Slick on the back and began walking away.

"Yep," was Slick's reply.

Next he passed Honey Winchester, a P.E. teacher at the elementary school. "Afternoon, ma'am."

"Ma'am? Aw, c'mon, I'm not that old, am I?" She put her hands on her hips and glared at him.

"I don't rightly know," Slick was sure however he answered that question, he would be in trouble. He tried to change the subject and said the first thing that came to mind. "Is it hot enough for you?"

She waved her hand in the air and said over her shoulder, "It's so hot

Satan must be right around the corner."

Slick nodded and began walking again. He pulled a red bandana handkerchief from his back pocket and wiped his brow as he waved to old man Hennepin who was sitting on a bench in front of the Second National Bank.

"Slick, how in the world are you?" The old man lifted his face as Slick passed in front of him.

"Doing all right. You?" He stuffed the bandana back in his pocket.

"I tell you what, it's too hot to do anything but breathe. If you go any faster than a mile per hour, you're gonna work up a sweat. Don't go doing nothing more than you have to on a day like this."

"I'll try to remember that." Slick kept walking. He looked down the street and saw a cherry red '54 Chevy truck coming his way. It went through a stop sign and had almost passed by Slick when the driver stepped on the brakes so hard it made the tires chirp.

"Hey, Slick!" The driver leaned across the passenger seat and hollered out the open window.

"Jackson." Slick stopped walking and waved. He saw Jack motioning for him to come closer, so he weaved through the parked cars on the street and walked to the truck.

"Listen, I'm trying to find that farm that sells those beeswax candles. You know the ones I'm talking about?"

"Yep." Slick nodded.

"I've been up one road and down another. I can't find it for the life of me. You know where it is?"

"Yep." Slick put his hands on the opening of the window and leaned in. "Take a left here." He pointed to the four-way stop ahead. "Then go another left and head out of town. It's on one of those old country roads – I can't remember the name of it." He stroked his chin. "It's something like Pope Lick, Lizard Lick, Chapstick, but that don't matter. As you approach it, you'll see one of those road signs like a sideways T. You know what I'm talking about?"

Jack nodded.

"Hit your clicker and slow your speed when you see the sign because the road will come up on you before you know it. Take a right on that road and go about a mile. The farm's on the left side of the road. You'll see the big red barn before you see the house."

"Will do, Slick. Thanks a bunch. You have a real good day."

Slick stepped back from the truck and waved as Jack drove off. Standing on the hot pavement for that short of a time made him feel like he was sweating from every pore in his body. He hopped the curb and headed for A Blue Million Books, two doors down. He stepped inside and felt instant relief.

Louetta Stafford came toward him. "You look like you're about cooked. I tell you what, it's so hot, I saw a bird pulling a worm out of the ground using potholders."

Slick looked down his nose at her. "Have you taken leave of your senses?"

"Well, I didn't mean literally. Sheesh. Some people are just too durn serious around here. How's Junebug put up with you anyhow?"

He shrugged. "She appreciates my good qualities."

"There's more than one?"

"Well you don't have to get snippety, Lou."

Lou playfully slapped his arm. "I'm just funning you. C'mon in." She took his arm. "You here to browse or just take advantage of the bought air?"

He looked sheepish. "The latter."

"All right. Sit yourself down in one of those comfy chairs. I'll get you a magazine."

"Naw, that's all right. I just wanted some momentary relief. I'm on a mission. I gotta get to it." He turned and headed for the door.

"All right then. I'll see you later."

"Thanks for the warning."

She looked sharply at him.

"Just funning you," he said with a grin before ducking out the door.

A shifty looking man was standing against the front of Fern & Moody's General Store, and as Slick approached, he pushed off and walked toward Slick.

"Holding up the wall there, dude?" Slick raised an eyebrow but kept walking.

The man stepped in front of him. "Maybe I am. And maybe I want all your money." He was breathing hard, and he brandished a gun.

The color drained from Slick's face. He felt his pants pockets and then his shirt pocket and stammered, "I, I don't have any cash on me." Several tense seconds passed before he added, "Will you take a check?"

The man scowled. "No, fool, I will *not* take a check. How stupid do you think I am?"

Slick regained his composure and leveled his gaze on the man. "Well, you're standing in the middle of town trying to rob me. I'd say you're one fish shy of a full string."

The man dropped the gun to his side and let out a breath as if a balloon had been popped. He seemed to shrink. "It's my mother's fault. I never was like this until I was born." He shook his head morosely and searched Slick's eyes. "I'm just so hungry, ya know?'

"Tell you what do. You wait right here, and I'll be out in a jiffy. We'll g'won up to the diner and you can wash dishes for your supper."

"Really? You'd do that? What for?"

Slick clapped his hand on the man's shoulder and looked him in the eye. "Because we ought to be more kind to one another in this world. You need help, and I can help, so that's what I'm gonna do." Slick took two steps then backtracked. Taking the gun from the man's limp hand, he said, "Why don't I just hold onto this for you?" He put the gun in his belt at the back of his trousers and pulled out his shirt to conceal it. Walking to the back of the store, he heard the whir of the meat slicer. Moody was standing next to it, a shocked expression on his face as he stared at his left hand, which was covered in blood. Slick hurried to him and saw that the man's index finger was missing.

"How in the world did you do that, Moody?"

Moody shrugged. "I was slicing beef roast, and I did like this." He put his hand up to the meat slicer and cut another finger off.

"Don't that beat all." Slick cut off the meat slicer. "I tell you what. If I were you, I wouldn't do that again." He reached for the phone to call 911.

Moody stared at his hand. "Yeah. I'm about to run out of fingers."

Slick hollered for Fern to bring a bucket of ice so they could preserve the fingers. Then he sat down next to Moody who looked to be in shock. He wanted to take the man's mind off his pain, so he said the first thing that came to mind. "Is it hot enough for ya?"

Don't Mess With Maude

She ain't no slow leak.

~Southern speculation

Stooped over and peering into the oven, Maude looked up when her husband, Claude, propped himself in the doorway looking sheepish. They'd been married for fifty-six years and she knew that look.

"I'm going up to the corner for a spell. I'll be back before long." His eyes were on his watch instead of his wife.

She stood up straight (as straight as a 75-year-old woman with osteoarthritis can stand), closing the oven door and giving him a long look. "Up to the corner means the Magnolia Bar, and before long means hours." She stood glaring at him, with her hands propped on her hips and her head shaking back and forth. She always shook and usually talked nonstop, whether anyone was around to hear or not. That's just the way she was—she talked and shook, talked and shook.

He stared blankly back, saying nothing, and then he walked up to her, taking her face in his hands and caressing it with his thumbs, trying in vain to stop the shaking and the anger in her eyes.

"Aw now, Maude," he crooned, "you'll be busy all afternoon cooking and won't even miss me. I'll be back in time for dinner. You don't think I'd miss Easter dinner, do you?"

His charm worked on her . . . like a charm. She softened and said, "The kids will be here at four."

Kissing her on her cheek, he said, "See you then, pretty lady."

"You'd better, Claude, you'd better!" she shouted after him. She went back to making potato salad, shaking and muttering about the uselessness of a man.

AT FOUR o'clock, the ham was out of the oven, the green beans were simmering on the stove, the potato salad was mounded high in her mother's cobalt blue bowl, the deviled eggs were arranged on the deviled egg plate they'd gotten as a wedding present, and the coconut cake stood proudly on the cake stand. Maude slid the cornstick pans into the oven just as she heard the voices at the front door.

"Yoohoo! Anybody home?"

Wiping her hands on her apron, she hurried to the door for hugs and kisses from her two daughters and their husbands. "Don't you look pretty." She clasped her hands together in delight. "Y'all look like Easter eggs in your bright dresses."

"Where's Daddy?" Callie, the oldest one, asked.

"He's up to the corner for a spell. Said he'd be back in time for dinner."

Maude ignored the look exchanged by her daughter and son-in-law.

"What you got there?" Maude asked Callie.

"Jell-O Easter eggs. Aren't they the cutest?"

Maude looked at the orange, red, and green jiggly egg-shaped Jell-O. "How'd you do that, Cal?" Her head shook in time with the quivering Jell-O eggs.

"With a mold. It's real easy."

"I brought tomato aspic, Mama," Jenna said, holding out the dish of deep red gelatin with carrots, celery, and green pepper sprinkled throughout.

"My favorite, darlin'. C'mon, bring everything back to the kitchen. Or better yet, g'won and put it on the dining room table. Everything's almost ready. Soon's the cornsticks are ready and your daddy gets home, we'll eat."

Fifteen minutes later, the cornsticks were out of the oven, but Claude wasn't home.

Twenty minutes after that, the cornsticks were lukewarm, and Claude still wasn't home.

"Y'ont I should go and get him, Mama?" Callie's husband, Campbell, asked.

Maude stood in the dining room doorway, shaking and surveying the table. It was set with her mama's good china, silverware, etched crystal glasses, and cloth napkins. She'd done the hydrangeas and peony centerpiece herself. It was Easter. And Claude was at the Mag bar.

Nobody was really surprised. He'd done it for just about every holiday except Christmas, and he'd only been home then because the bar was closed on Christmas. He knew she spent days preparing for the meal. He knew the family would be there. He knew how important it was to her, yet more often than not, he was either late or missed the meal altogether because he was up at the bar boozing.

Campbell touched her tissue-paper-crinkled arm. "I can just run up and bring him on back, okay?"

She patted his hand, and her eyes lit up. A smile spread across her face, and she must've looked a bit wicked because Campbell stepped back, his mouth shaped in an O.

"No thank you, Campbell. If Claude can't find his way back home in time for Easter dinner, we'll just take it to him."

The family gaped at her.

Thirty minutes later, Maude, decked out in her Easter bonnet, marched down the sidewalk, shaking and muttering, with her daughters and their husbands trailing behind. Everyone's arms were laden with dishes. Maude opened the door to the Mag Bar and stepped inside, pausing to allow her eyes to adjust to the dim light inside. Once she had her bearings, she took her picnic basket full of china and silver and headed for the biggest table in the center of the room. She pulled a white linen tablecloth from the basket and covered the scratched, sticky table.

Next, she set the table with the silverware, china, and crystal. She took the centerpiece from Campbell, as the girls placed the food around the table. When everything was pretty as a magazine spread, Marie stood up straight, smoothing her dress with her hands, and called across the room to her husband, who was sitting at the bar staring at her, along with everyone else.

In her sweetest voice possible, she said, "Claude, would you care to join us?"

Claude didn't miss another holiday meal after that. Ever.

TAKE IT, TAKE IT, TAKE IT!

There's no fool like an old fool.

~Southern conjecture

Back in the day, Clive Pierce was a farmer and a tradesman. He prided himself on being able to get the best of every deal he made. One afternoon, a gentleman had come to the farm looking to buy a pig. The men dickered for about ten minutes then shook hands. The man took his new pig with him and Clive pocketed some cash.

Later that afternoon, Clive's wife, Martha, came out of the house looking for him. She realized it had been quite some time since she'd seen him.

She walked into the barn, where she found her son Billy. "You seen your pa?"

He cocked his head. "No, actually, now that you mention it, it's been a few hours." Billy followed her out of the barn and to the pigpen, where they found Edna Earl, feeding the pigs.

"You seen your pa?"

She put her hands on her hips. "It's been a few hours."

Martha nodded, turned on her heel, and headed down the hill, her son and daughter following.

They walked toward the fields and she saw her two sons, Freddie and Eddie, standing ramrod straight, leaning slightly into one another, in the field next to the barn. Claude Davis, a neighbor, stood nearby with his hands in his pockets, eating an apple and looking from one man to the other as they fought.

"You know what you are? You're a gross ignoramus." Freddie started to turn around but changed course and faced Eddie again. "And that's 144 times worse than an ordinary ignoramus."

"Why don't you put your money where your mouth is?"

"Boys, what in tarnation is going on back here?" Martha stopped next to Eddie and clapped him on the shoulder. "What's got you two so riled up?"

"Mama, how long I been growing mushmelons?" Eddie jammed his hands on his hips. "And how long has *he* been growing them?" He hitched his thumb in his brother's direction.

"Oh, prolly about the same amount of time, I reckon."

"And which one of us grows the best crop every dern season?"

"Oh, whichever one has the biggest mushmelon, I reckon."

"Well, I propose a contest. The Best Crop Contest. And we'll let daddy be the judge on," he thought for a moment and then finished his thought, "August first."

"Speaking of your daddy, you boys seen him lately?"

The boys shook their heads and went back to arguing. Martha, Edna Earl, and Billy kept walking. Down the hill they went, toward the sorghum mill. And there he was. He had a mule hooked up going around and around grinding cane into sorghum, and he walking alongside the animal, talking to it. Martha picked up speed, determined to give him a piece of her mind.

When she got closer, she heard what he was saying to the mule: "I took fifty, shoulda got a hundred. I took fifty, shoulda got a hundred . . . "

CLIVE PIERCE sat in the rocking chair on the lawn of his home, slowly rocking back and forth, listening to the birds sing and the wind rustle the leaves on the trees. It was a quiet summer day in Goose Pimple Junction until he saw Jimmy, the grocery delivery boy, pedaling toward him from town.

"Afternoon, son. Hireyew?"

"Doing all right, sir. Doing all right." Jimmy's "all right" came out like "aw rot."

Clive squinted up at the almost grown man. "What's your name again?"

"Jimmy Pierce, sir." He swallowed hard.

"Pierce." Clive stroked his chin. "We related?"

"Don't rightly know, sir." His hands went in his pockets, and he kicked softly at the grass.

There was a gleam in Clive's eye. "Do you like to drink whiskey?"

"Yeah." Jimmy nodded sheepishly.

"Do you like the women?" Clive's forehead wrinkled, his eyebrows rising slightly.

"Well, yeah." Jimmy's cheeks blossomed with two red patches.

Clive sat up and leaned toward Jimmy. "Do you like to bet on the ponies from time to time?"

"Yeah." Jimmy hung his head.

Clive's chin jutted out, and he whispered, "Do you like a nice cigar from time to time?"

"Uh huh."

Clive kicked his heel up and slapped his knee in the air. "Come quick, Martha! We have a full-blooded Pierce here."

They were still laughing about that when Edna Earl, Clive's grown daughter came out into the yard.

"Edna Earl," Jimmy said, "I was actually here to talk to you."

"Oh?" She cocked her head.

"You know that land you have up on Buttermilk Pike?"

"Yeah, I know it. Daddy here gave it to me."

"You wouldn't be interested in selling it, would you?"

"Well, now, I might entertain an offer or two."

Jimmy sidled closer to the woman. "How much you think it's worth?"

"Oh, about as much as someone's willing to pay." Her smile was genuine, but she had learned the art of trading from her daddy, and she wasn't about to tip her hand.

Jimmy chuckled. "True, that. Well – " he reached into his pocket and pulled out a golf-sized pencil and a scrap of paper, "would you take this?" He scribbled something on the paper and handed it to Edna Earl.

She took it, looked at the number he'd written, and then said, "That and ten thousand more."

He shook his head and walked away but returned a few days later. Clive was in his usual spot in the front yard, and he called for his daughter to come outside when he saw Jimmy approaching the house.

"I've decided to meet your price." He was sweating under the noon sun and wiped his brow.

Edna Earl shielded her eyes against the bright sun. "Well, that's a shame, because my price has gone up another five thousand."

Jimmy walked away shaking his head.

This went on four or five times, until he returned one day with fire in his eyes. He handed her a slip of paper and said, "This is my final offer."

She scrunched up her mouth and handed the paper to her father. Clive looked at it. Then he reached into his pocket and pulled out a stubby pencil. He wrote something on the paper and handed it back to his daughter.

She looked down at the scrap and saw he'd scribbled: *Take it take it take it!*

SAY YES, TESS!

You took as long as a month of Sundays.

~Southern hyperbole

Jack and Tess were having a picnic at their favorite spot on a hill overlooking Goose Creek. Tess loved the old trees and the wild flowers that dotted the area. She had just finished eating a chicken wrap, and she was taking a sip of sweet tea when Jack said, "Let's get married."

Too much tea went down her throat in one gulp, and she coughed for several seconds, her hand on her Adam's apple. Finally, she choked out, "Excuse me?"

"I think we should get married." He said it as if he were reporting the weather.

"Um . . . no." She began cleaning up the wrappers and napkins.

"Come again?"

"No, thank you." She smiled disingenuously.

"Well, well why not?" His back became ramrod straight.

"Jack, you know I love you – "

"So let's get married."

She held out her index finger. "Number one, I don't think a marriage proposal should be made so lightly. I'm not asking you to wear shining armor and gallop up on a horse, but I'm not about to take a marriage proposal seriously when the question could just as easily have been 'Would you like pie?'"

He shook his head. "We don't have any pie."

She rolled her eyes. "It was just an example."

"What's number two?"

"We've only been seeing each other for a short time. It's too fast."

The subject was changed that day, but Jack persisted. A few days later, he took her fishing. It was summertime, and the trees were lush and full; the sun shone on the water like diamonds. Jack fished and Tess watched, enjoying the scenery, the nice day, and being with Jack. He pulled his line from the water and reeled it in. Walking together to another spot, he said over his shoulder to her, "Marry me."

"No," was her quick response.

He just shook his head.

She spread out her hands. "Jack, you have a fishing pole in your hand, for heaven's sake."

"So?"

Soon after that, they were playing Scrabble, and he spelled out MARRY ME on the game board.

She scowled at him. "You cheater. There's no way you just happened to get those tiles."

He simply shrugged his shoulders and said, "Well?"

She had to wait several turns, but she finally got the right tiles to make the word NO.

Tess was walking to work one day when she saw single letters written in chalk on each square of the sidewalk ahead spelling out, MARRY ME, PLEASE? The please was written in extra heavy chalk. One square of sidewalk had a whole message written on it: I LOVE YOU A TON except the last two words ran together and looked like ATON.

She laughed out loud and pulled out her cell phone, first taking a picture of the sidewalk message, and then texting Jack: *No.*

His immediate reply: *Ah, come on, boo. why not? we're perfect for each other.*

You're very cute, but it's too soon.

The next day, she got a letter in the mail reminiscent of the threatening letter she'd gotten just a month before. Jack had imitated that letter by also writing the message in cutout magazine letters:

PLeAsE

mARRy

ME

That night, she climbed in bed and turned out the lights. As she lay there, glow in the dark letters appeared on her ceiling over her bed with the now familiar message: MARRY ME.

"Oh, for heaven's sake," she said to the dark room.

Her text notification chimed. She picked up her phone and saw *Well?* on the screen.

She typed, *How did you know I just saw your message?*

I've been sitting outside your house for 30 minutes waiting for the light to go out.

Then another message rolled in: *What say you?*

Too soon.

There was no response.

She lay there in the dark thinking about Jack. She loved him more than was probably sane and couldn't imagine life without him. He was everything she'd ever wanted in a man. So why wasn't she saying yes? Tess loved his sense of humor, and she laughed more with him than she ever had with anyone else, but she had a nagging feeling that she was ahead of him in the falling in love department. And they'd only been together for a few months. She fell asleep thinking, *It's too soon, and he's not taking this seriously. Marriage isn't a game.*

As if Jack read her mind, he upped his game. He came to her house one night and not so nonchalantly asked, "So what is your ring size?"

She mockingly swooned. "You're so romantic."

He put his hands in the air. "I can't get you a ring if I don't know what size to get."

"And you can't surprise me if you ask obvious questions like that."

"Okay. How about this for a surprise?" He pulled a ring box from his jacket pocket and opened the lid. A two-carat sparking diamond ring sat in the cushion.

She gasped and her hand flew to her mouth. "Jack," was all she could say.

He got down on one knee and said, "Tess Tremaine, will you *please* marry me?"

She got down on her knees so she could look him in the eye. "I'll give it some serious consideration." Then she kissed him.

A week later, she still had not made up her mind. As she walked to work, an unusual number of people were walking toward her on the sidewalk, and they all had on the same T-shirt in an unusual shade of coral. As she approached the bookstore, a dozen people mingled out front, all wearing the same coral T-shirt.

Then she heard someone say, "She's coming." They suddenly turned their backs to her and formed a line, shoulder to shoulder, so that their shirts spelled out MARRY ME, TESS! The same people who had passed her on the sidewalk a minute ago all stood on the opposite street corner. They too had their backs to her, and each of their shirts said: SAY YES, TESS!

As everyone began clapping, she hurried inside and ran smack into Jack, who was waiting just inside the door. He too was wearing a coral T-shirt that said: SAY YES, TESS.

"You've got the whole town involved in your proposal now?"

"Well, I wasn't doing so hot on my own," he joked, as Louetta and Pickle, also wearing coral T-shirts and big smiles, came from the back room.

Louetta walked toward them with her finger pointed at Tess. "Tess Tremaine, you won't find a better man than this one here," her finger moved from Tess's direction to Jack's and back again, "and you know it. I swan, if you don't hurry up and say yes, I'm gonna steal him out from under you."

"And I might just let her too." Jack put his arm around Louetta and squeezed her into his side.

"Well, then there's only one thing I can say." Tess began walking toward the back room.

Jack spoke up. "So that's a yes?"

She stopped walking and turned around to face him. Walking back to stand before him, she cupped his cheek and said, "I hope you two will be very happy." Then she turned on her heel and walked away.

FOR THREE days, everywhere she went, someone had on a coral T-shirt with SAY YES, TESS! written on the back. And it seemed that everywhere she looked, she saw the same message written:

with magnets on the refrigerator

with a glass pen on the diner's front window

inside her menu at the Silly Goose

on her paper cup from the Muffin Man

spelled out with green peppers on a pizza

on the table spelled out in Cheerios

One day, every person she ran into handed her a flyer that said: SAY YES, TESS! By the end of the day, she had a ream or more of flyers. She tried to form Team Tess and have them spread the message, GET BACK, JACK, but everyone was on Jack's side.

Finally, on a hot day in late August, she was gathering her things to go home when Louetta handed her a hard copy of *The Princess Bride*. When she looked quizzically at Lou, her friend bobbed her head at the book and said, "Open it." Inside, she found a note:

Twu wuv...you are my twu wuv...if you were a book, i'd read you all night. now go to Slick & Junebug's Diner.

"What in the Sam Hill – "

Louetta folded her arms. "You best be getting on to the diner, missy."

Tess walked out into the soup that used to be air and felt like she waded down the sidewalk to Slick & Junebug's Diner. Walking into the restaurant, she thought about the first time, and all of the subsequent times, she and Jack had come here to eat. She sat down at the counter next to Earl.

Clive was on Earl's other side, and he leaned over his friend to tell Tess, "You're slower than a herd of turtles stampeding through peanut butter, you know that? What's the matter with you? When you gonna say yes to that man?"

Tess raised her eyebrows. "Seriously? He sent me over here to get a lecture from you gentlemen?"

Junebug stepped up to the counter, holding a paper napkin. "No, he did not. He sent you here for this."

The napkin said:

I love you more than a fat kid loves cake. Now kindly go to the Muffin Man.

Junebug handed her a cupcake with the word YES spelled out on top in frosting. "Give him this, sugar. Put the man out of his misery."

She walked to the Muffin Man thinking about the first time she and Jack ever talked to one another in that very coffee shop. At the counter, the barista handed her a paper cup with lemonade tea inside. Written on the outside was:

You're the cream in my coffee, the sugar in my tea. I sure wish you would marry me. Next stop: The Silly Goose.

She just shook her head and headed for the Silly Goose, thinking about all the romantic dinners they'd had at that restaurant. Inside, the hostess handed her a candle with a slip of paper curled around it. She unrolled it and read:

YOU ARE THE LIGHT TO MY CANDLE. NOW PLEASE GO TO FERN & MOODY'S.

Fern & Moody's General Store was the specialty store where they always got their picnic lunches. At Fern & Moody's, she was given an apple with a note tied to a string, which was attached to the stem. The note said:

You are the apple to my pie. See? There is pie! Next stop: The Second National Bank.

Tess walked to the bank, thinking about the robbery that occurred there in 1932 and how that one event brought her and Jack together. The main teller was Dee Dee, a dour, grumpy woman who always wore a sour expression.

"Ya ain't gonna get rich with that'n, that's for sure." She handed Tess a bank envelope. Inside was a penny and a note:

You're the copper to my penny. If I had a penny for every person I've met who makes me feel the way you do, I'd have exactly one cent. Marry me, woman! If you're still unsure, please go to the Pure Oil Gas Station.

The gas station. That frightening day when she and Martha Maye were trapped came rushing to her thoughts. Then she remembered flying out the door and into Jack's arms. Jeb Crowley, the owner of the filling station, was washing a windshield in the full-service lane while the car's tank filled with gas. He looked up as Tess approached and shook his head.

"I don't have the foggiest idea what that man is up to, but he said to give you this." He reached into his pocket and pulled out an object wrapped in paper. She unwrapped it and found a spark plug and a note that said:

You are the spark to my plug. Okay, I'm reaching on this one. Help me out and say yes.

Tess looked up at Jeb, and he said, "He said to tell you if you still won't say yes – and woman, why you wouldn't say yes is beyond me – but he said to tell you to go to Doc's Hardware."

She walked in a fog to the hardware store. *How can anyone be sure in just a couple of months?*

Inside the store, Doc gave her a box, and inside it was a small metal spring with a tag attached that said:

You're the spring to my step. Now spring on over to the Gazebo.

Walking toward the gazebo in the town green, she saw that the area was practically deserted. Her eyes went to the gazebo, and there stood Jack with a huge smile on his face and Ezzie at his feet. Behind them, she noticed the gazebo was filled with deep blue hydrangeas – her favorite.

Jack was wearing tan dress slacks, a light pink button-down Oxford shirt, and loafers. He looked good enough to eat. Ezzie saw Tess and let out a bark, her tail wagging and thumping on the floor of the gazebo. Jack and Tess's eyes locked as she walked toward him. He took her hand and led her into the gazebo. She had never seen such beautiful hydrangeas, and they covered almost every surface. He'd made sure there was room enough for two on the bench. They sat down, Jack still holding onto her hand.

"Jack, I – "

"Me first," he interrupted.

She nodded.

"I know it's only been a couple of months. But I know I've never felt this way about anyone before. When I'm with you, I'm the happiest I've ever been. When we're apart, all I can think about is seeing you again. I want you all the time, Tess. I want us to be together. I want us to spend the rest of our lives making each other happy. And I *know* we will be. Tess, I want you to be my wife. Please say you'll marry me. Please say yes." Ezzie's cold nose bumped her leg.

Without hesitation, Tess said, "Yes."

In one fluid motion, he stood, pulling her into his arms. Still holding on tight, he yelled over her shoulder, "She said yes!"

People came out of every nook and cranny, applauding.

Jack and Tess stood laughing and holding and kissing each other. When he broke the kiss, he looked at her, nose-to-nose, and said, "You did just say yes, right?"

Holding on tight to his hand, she went to the gazebo's entrance and shouted, "I said yes!"

TALL
TALE

ONE BAD APPLE

1
THE INTERVIEW

I was born at night, but not last night.

~Johnny Butterfield

Butterbean Applewhite ushered Johnny Butterfield from the front door to the kitchen where her grandmother, Louetta Stafford, sat at the table talking with Jackson Wright, Tess Tremaine, Pickle Culpepper, and her mother, Martha Maye Applewhite. Just a few hours before, Tess and Martha Maye had been held hostage, and the kitchen was abuzz.

Martha Maye jumped up. "Have a seat, Trooper Butterfield, how about I cut you a nice big slice of chocolate cake?" She smiled up at the state trooper. He stood six foot five, and the phrase tall, dark, and handsome didn't do the man justice. His biceps stretched the confines of his shirtsleeves, and when his dark eyes landed on Martha Maye, she blushed.

"Just Johnny will be fine. And thank you, ma'am." He switched to his Elvis voice. "Thank ya ver' much." He forgot for a few seconds that he and Martha Maye weren't alone. Martha Maye was a pretty woman with just a little too much weight attached to her hips and thighs. But that didn't stop Johnny from wanting to stare at her. Finally pulling his eyes from hers, he said to the group, "I stopped by to tell y'all that John Ed has resigned his position as police chief. He's under review for hindering an investigation."

"Who's gonna be police chief?" Louetta asked.

"Um . . . the position's open. And they're taking applications." He darted a glance at Martha Maye, who met his eyes and then took her gaze to the floor.

Jackson Wright stood and pulled Tess to her feet. "Well, folks, it's been a long day. I'm going to see Tess home now."

Tess went to the state trooper and took his hand. "Trooper Butterfield, thank you for all you did today. We appreciate it more than we can say."

"Aw, just doing my duty, ma'am, and call me Johnny."

"Call *me* Tess." She smiled up at him. "Thank you, Johnny," Tess touched his shoulder to punctuate her thanks, while she laced the fingers on her other hand through Jack's.

"Goodnight, y'all!" Jack and Tess said in unison, leaving the kitchen with Louetta at their heels. Jack looked at her with a smile in his eyes and whispered, "You're turning into a Southern belle already."

"Night, you two," Martha Maye said, almost as an afterthought. She busied herself wiping the countertop and sneaking glances at Johnny.

Johnny turned to the lanky teenager who was leaning against the kitchen counter. "Pickle, I'd say you saved the day, son. You ever thought about a job in law enforcement?"

Pickle's face flushed red. "Uh . . . no, sir. I'm still in high school."

Johnny studied the kid to see if he might be pulling his leg, but he looked perfectly serious. "I meant after high school."

Pickle scratched his head, leaving the hair at the top of his head standing up.

"Oh. Wull...nope, can't say I ever thought that."

"I think you'd be a natural. You let me know if you're ever interested in looking into police work as a career."

"Aw, I don't know..."

"Just keep it in mind." Johnny gave a lingering look to Martha Maye and then pushed his hands through his hair. "Well folks, it's been a day and a half today. I'm gonna get."

Martha Maye jumped to her feet. "Oh, don't rush off . . . Johnny." She smiled up at him.

Johnny shoved the last bite of chocolate cake in his mouth and handed her the plate. "I expect I better. Technically, I'm still on duty. But I hope to see y'all real soon." He put on his trooper hat and adjusted it in the front, adding, "If the good Lord's willing and the creek don't rise."

A WEEK later:

"Well, Trooper Butterfield, I see your record is exemplary, but I'm just concerned about your experience as a leader." Mayor Buck Lyons sat back in his chair and laced his fingers over his stomach. He was leading Johnny's interview for police chief with the city councilmen.

"Aw, Buck, you flap your gums just to hear yourself talk," Clive said.

"Now, Clive, we're conducting business here. I'd appreciate it if you'd call me Mayor."

"Well, I'd just appreciate it if somebody would call me to dinner. Boy, I've known you since you were no bigger 'n a beef roast, and I'll kindly call you what I want. Stop taking yourself so seriously." He turned to Johnny. "Does your . . . " he put his fingers up for air quotes, "*lack of experience* disturb you, young man?"

"No, sir, it doesn't. I have a degree in criminal justice, I've learned a lot by paying attention on the job, and I can think on my feet. I'm confident I'd do a good job as police chief. I wouldn't apply if I didn't think I could do the job."

"The work entails a good bit more than your average crime fighting skills, Trooper Butterfield. We try to keep expenses low. I know John Ed replaced brake pads on the cruisers more than once. He also wasn't above cleaning a toilet or sitting on dispatch if need be. I — "

"I take your point. I'm no prima don. I do what it takes, no matter what."

"Uh, isn't that prima donna?" Clive leaned in.

"Wull . . . yeah . . . but I'm a guy. I ain't no Donna." He grinned.

"Duly noted." Buck looked at Johnny over his reading glasses then at the others at the table. "I'll have to say I was right impressed with the way you handled that kidnapping situation the other day. You were confident, authoritative, and you got the job done."

"Thank you, sir. But you have good men on the force here. I was just backup."

"You were more than that. We were liable to end up with someone shot. I credit you with getting the job done and nobody ending up seriously hurt."

"Thank you again. I don't like to toot my own horn — "

"Well, an interview for police chief sure is the time and place if ever there was one," Clive said. "G'won." He waved his hand in the air. "Toot."

Johnny's face turned serious. "I can think on my feet. I don't get rattled, and I don't back down. I'm able to size up a scene, and I'm proud to say I haven't had one unsuccessful outcome of a bad situation."

"Do you mind if I ask about your personal life?" Mayor Lyons said.

"Ask away."

"You married?"

"Nope. Never been. But I hope to someday."

"Got someone serious, do you?" There was a gleam in Clive's eye.

"No. Just hopes and dreams."

"Don't we all." Buck pushed back from the table and addressed the other interviewers." Okay, y'all, anyone have any other questions for Trooper Butterfield?" Everyone looked at each other, but no one spoke. The mayor again addressed Johnny. "That's it for now, then. We'll inform you of our decision soon's we know it. Thank you for coming in."

2
SEE AND BE SEEN

What's a Southern girl's mating call? I've got season tickets!

~ Caledonia Culpepper

aledonia Culpepper was the picture of beauty as she walked past the shops on Main Street. The late August sun beaming down made her blonde hair brighter than usual. In her early forties, with a sleeveless yellow sundress and white sandals, her hair falling softly at her shoulders, and a bright smile on her heart-shaped face, she was a head turner. And she was on a mission. She pulled open the bookstore's heavy wooden door and glided inside.

The first person she saw was her son, Pickle. She frowned at his wrinkled T-shirt that said, BUCKLE UP. IT MAKES IT HARDER FOR ALIENS TO SNATCH YOU OUT OF YOUR CAR.

She propped a hand on her hip. "Pickle, why're you wearing that shirt out in public? It's wrinkled."

Without skipping a beat he said, "*You're* wrinkled." His face suddenly showed horror as he realized what he'd said. His hand went up to his mouth while his eyes grew big as saucers.

Caledonia's mouth flew open, and she gasped, her hand going to the pearls around her neck.

"He didn't mean it like that, Callie." Louetta stepped from behind the cash register. "We've got a running joke around here. It's like a game. Say someone says something is impossible . . . the other person will say, 'You're impossible'. Or . . . I might say, 'That shelf is dusty.' And someone else would say, 'You're dusty.' See? All in fun."

Caledonia gave her son a suspicious look, while he stood there looking as if he were facing a firing squad. Finally, she pointed a finger at him. "You watch out, youngin'. Someday I just might have to turn you into relish." But she smiled at him to let him know she was teasing.

Pickle exhaled visibly, and Caledonia turned when Martha Maye came in from the back room.

"Just the woman I wanted to see." Caledonia walked up to her. "Did y'all hear?"

"Hear what?"

"That state trooper. You know, the one who rescued y'all." Martha Maye nodded and her cheeks flushed a slight red. "The councilmen and Buck are interviewing him as we speak."

"For police chief?" She stood up a little straighter.

"Don't you know it." Caledonia's head bobbed up and down. "I saw the way you looked at him that day. I thought maybe you should know he was in town." She grabbed Martha Maye's hand. "C'mon, let's you and me just happen to walk past the police station."

"I, I, I can't just leave the store," Martha Maye sputtered.

"I don't know why in the world not." Lou came toward them. "I can take care of things while you're gone for a bit." She smiled and winked at Caledonia. "That's the best idea you've had since you brought that Jell-O salad to the potluck dinner."

"True love cannot be denied." Caledonia pulled Martha Maye to the door.

"Wait a minute!" Martha Maye stopped walking. "I need to go put some lipstick on and powder my nose."

Caledonia studied her. "Oh, all right. But you best not take too long. We don't want to miss him."

"And put some color on your cheeks too," Louetta hollered at her daughter's back.

Two minutes later, the two women were casually, but with purpose, walking toward the police station. "What are we gonna do, Callie? We can't just stand around outside. We'll look like a pair of streetwalkers."

"I've got that all worked out." Caledonia looped her arm through Martha Maye's. "I got a parking ticket last week, and we're going in to pay it. You just happen to be with me, that's all. Perfectly innocent."

"But I won't know what to say to him. And I really shouldn't be making goo-goo eyes at a man until the divorce is final."

"It won't hurt to see and be seen." They stopped in front of Miss Penny's Dress Shop and looked in the window. Caledonia looked at Martha Maye through the window's reflection. "If we time it right, we'll be there when the meeting breaks up." She looked at her watch. "Bernadette told me the interview was starting at one o'clock. We figured about forty-five minutes ought to do it." Caledonia saw Penny inside looking at them, so they began walking again.

"That woman talks so much, I'll bet her tongue is sunburned."

"Who? Penny?"

Caledonia nodded.

"Weren't y'all schoolmates?"

Caledonia shot Martha Maye a look. "Yes, but she's two years older than me, thank you very much."

"And isn't she on your PTA board?"

"Unfortunately, she is. I think she's made it her mission to make my life miserable. But, hey, speaking of school, I heard you've got some good news."

Martha Maye looked surprised. "You mean about the job? They just offered it to me yesterday. How on earth did you hear so quick?"

Caledonia had a smug look on her face. "I'm PTA president. I find out all sorts of things by hanging around over at that school. You're gonna like teaching first graders. I'm so excited you're gonna be there."

"I'm getting pretty excited too." Martha Maye hugged her friend's arm.

"It's all coming together for you, girl, and I couldn't be happier for you."

"Next order of business is to find a place for Butterbean and me to live. I'd like to rent a small house. You know of anything like that for rent right now?"

Caledonia shook her head. "No, next order of business is to remind Mr. Johnny Butterfield that the lovely Martha Maye Applewhite lives in this town."

They were almost to the police station. Martha Maye tightened her grip on her friend's arm. "Oh, Caledonia, I don't know how I let you talk me into this."

"Twue wuv . . . " Caledonia mimicked the line from *The Princess Bride* and Martha Maye nudged her with her shoulder. Caledonia dabbed her lips with a little lipstick as they turned onto the sidewalk leading to the front door of the police station.

"Well, if it's true love, it shouldn't need any help. I think we should just turn around and — "

"Too late. Look who's coming outta that door." Caledonia nodded her head at the front door.

And suddenly, there he was, looking better than any man had a right to. His blue suit and red tie took Martha Maye's breath away. He spoke first as he neared them.

"Martha Maye, is that you?"

"Johnny!" She stammered and then said, "I mean, I mean, Trooper Butterfield — "

"Nope, you had it right the first time. Johnny will do fine. Besides, I'm hoping it won't be Trooper Butterfield much longer."

Caledonia was enjoying watching the exchange between the two. Both of their faces had colored upon first sight of each other. She could tell Martha Maye's mouth was dry as a cotton field, and she noticed Johnny wiping his hands on the sides of his trousers. Neither one could take their eyes off the other.

"Wh-what do you mean?"

"I was just in there interviewing for the position of police chief."

Martha Maye looked like she'd just swallowed a bug, but Caledonia saved the day.

"Congratulations, Johnny, that's great news. Isn't that great news, Martha Maye?"

She looked at Caledonia as if she was just now remembering she was there. "Yes. Yes, it certainly is. I swan, where are my manners? Caledonia Culpepper, this is Troo — " she quickly corrected herself "– Johnny Butterfield, future GPJPD chief." She flashed a confident smile.

Johnny held up a hand. "No congratulations just yet. I don't quite have the job. Just call me Johnny." He stuck out his hand.

"And I'm very pleased to meet you, *future* Chief Butterfield." Caledonia shook his hand vigorously, and her suspicions of his nervousness were proven. She felt like she needed a hanky to wipe the moisture off her hand, but she kept her impeccable manners and her smile in place.

"Johnny, this is Pickle's mama. You remember Pickle?"

"I sure do. I'm mighty proud of that boy and his quick thinking. I told him he ought to consider a career in law enforcement."

"You did?" Her jaw went slack.

"I did."

"Well. Trying to train him in the ways of the law might be like teaching a rock to swim, bless his heart."

"Oh, I don't know. He's got natural instincts. The rest he can learn." There was an awkward silence that Johnny finally broke. "So . . . what brings y'all to the police station?"

"I'm a law breaker, and I'm here to pay my debt." Caledonia worked hard to make her face blank.

"You're going to jail?" Johnny looked incredulous.

"No, no. Nothing like that." She waved her hands in the air. "I'm just paying some parking tickets, and Martha Maye came along to keep me company."

"I sure am glad she did." Johnny beamed at Martha Maye, who picked at some lint on her sleeve.

After another awkward silence, Johnny said, "Y'all wouldn't know of any little houses for rent, would you?"

"I was just asking Caledonia the same thing, Johnny. Butterbean and I are looking too. I think it's time we went out on our own."

"You're looking at the newest teacher of the Robert E. Lee Elementary School." Caledonia proudly patted her friend on the arm.

"Congratulations, Martha Maye. That's wonderful news. What grade will you be teaching?"

A man and a woman started up the sidewalk toward the police station and Johnny, Caledonia, and Martha Maye stepped apart to allow them through.

"Hey, Pete. Hey, Tallulah. Hire y'all?" Martha Maye introduced them to Johnny and Caledonia and then asked, "What brings y'all to the police station?"

Pete's wide grin covered his face as he looked at Tallulah. "Not the police station. We're going to the courthouse to get a marriage license."

That brought squeals from the women, and Johnny shook hands with Pete.

"Congratulations, y'all. Bless your hearts," Martha Maye said.

"Thank you." Pete nodded to the ladies. "We believe we've made . . . how do you say it? A right good choice."

"I expect you have." Martha Maye kissed Pete on the cheek, causing his face to turn bright red.

With a wave, Pete and Talullah walked toward city hall, hand in hand.

Martha Maye turned toward Johnny. "Are you coming to Apple Day?"

"If I'm still a state trooper, I'll be working it. Maybe I'll see you there."

"May be." She put special emphasis on "be," smiled, and held his gaze for a moment before turning toward the police station with Caledonia. Martha Maye turned around and called out, "I just know you'll get the job. And you'll be great."

"From your lips to God's ears," Johnny called back.

3
OLD MAN SHAW

Eating brains don't make you a scientist.

~Clive Pierce

A week later, Johnny was back for his third interview with the councilmen and the mayor. They explained that they liked him for the job but some still had reservations about his age. They were fifteen minutes into the interview when Bernadette stuck her head in the door.

"Mayor, we got us a situation. Vernice Anderson up in Gnaw Bone reported seeing that fool, old man Shaw, brandishing a firearm."

"Let me guess. She said he's armed and dangerous?" Mayor Lyons said with a grin, eliciting snickers from the others.

Bernadette was all business. "Yeah, kinda. Turns out he has a record. He's been in the big house for assault and battery." She propped her hand on her hip. "You know, some folks just plain don't have the sense of an animal cracker. Why, I — "

"Bernadette!"

She nearly jumped to attention.

"What's the situation?"

"That's the thing. I don't know." She let out an exasperated sigh. "I sent Hank up there along with Northington, but I haven't heard pea turkey squat from either one. I called Vernice back, and she said there's been shots fired."

Buck looked at Johnny. His eyebrows rose up over his eyeglasses. "What would *you* do if *you* were police chief?"

"I reckon I'd go out there myself."

"Then get. We'll call it on the job interviewing. I'll go with you and watch from the cruiser."

The councilmen kept their seats. Clive propped his feet up on the table and reared back in his chair. "Y'all let us know if we can do anything."

JOHNNY TORE up Gnaw Bone Road in his state trooper vehicle, gravel spitting in his wake. Buck held on for dear life in the passenger seat. They'd brought Officer Skeeter Duke with them, but he seemed unconcerned in the back seat.

"Good Lord, boy. Where'd you learn to drive?" Buck asked.

"State training, sir."

"I gotta hand it to them. They trained you well. You're fast, but you're good." In a smaller voice, he added, "I hope."

"Don't you worry, Mayor. I'll get us there in one piece." Johnny gripped the steering wheel, never taking his eyes off the road.

Buck laughed nervously. "I'm alternating between chewing buttonholes and having the time of my life."

"This is almost as good as a high-speed pursuit." Skeeter clapped Johnny on the shoulder.

The car radio squawked. "Trooper Butterfield, we got a call from the Goose Pimple Junction dispatcher, asking us to relay a message to you."

"Go ahead."

"The situation you're en route to has escalated. Apparently, Officer Hank Beanblossom approached the subject to take the gun away from him, and now there's a hostage situation. The whole force is at the scene."

"Roger that." Johnny was quiet for a moment. Then he asked Buck, "Is there a way around the back of the property? Some way we can get in without being seen?"

"Sure. Take a left up here at the four-way. And then another left."

Johnny followed his instructions.

"Now ease up on the gas. The road will sneak up on you. " They slowed to 15 mph. When they reached a narrow gravel lane, Buck pointed. "Here. Go up this road. It'll take us to the Everly's place. They're backdoor neighbors to old man Shaw. His farm long ago gave way to a subdivision. They're the closest to him from the back."

Johnny, Skeeter, and Buck snuck through a cornfield and came upon the back of the Shaw house. The trooper eased past an old tractor, peeked around the corner of the house, and saw four GPJ police cruisers, all with their lights blaring. All the officers were behind their cruisers, their guns aimed at the house. Then a nasally voice boomed out, "Y'all just go on about your business, and I'll let this officer go. I don't want to cause nobody any harm, but I'll do it if it means protecting what's mine. Now y'all get."

"That's old man Shaw," Skeeter whispered, and Buck nodded in agreement.

Johnny hitched his head toward the back of the house, turned, and headed back the way they'd come. When they reached the back porch, he turned to Skeeter. "I need you to create a diversion. Anything within reason and that won't get anyone killed. Do it in – " he looked at his watch " – two minutes and thirty-five seconds, starting . . ." Both men looked at their watches. " . . . now."

Skeeter hightailed it around to the other side of the house.

Johnny turned to Buck. "You, stay right here."

"Hold it! Where are you going?"

"Inside to stop all this foolishness." Johnny quietly turned the knob on the door and gently eased it open. A kitchen floorboard squeaked, and a cat darted out of the room as Johnny stepped inside. He made his way through the house to the front room where he parted lace curtains – once white, but now a grimy gray – with his hand in order to peek out the window at the scene.

The scraggly yard was littered with a few squirrel carcasses, and Allen Ray Shaw stood on his front porch behind Officer Beanblossom. He had the officer's arm jerked behind him and was holding it with one hand and a pistol to Hank's head with his other hand. A revolver – Johnny guessed it belonged to Hank – lay a few feet from the men. Johnny checked his watch and removed his revolver, taking it off safety.

"You got a license for that thing?" A voice boomed out from behind one of the cruisers.

"Sure I do. And don't be thinking you're gonna take my gun away from me. I got rights. It's in the fifth amendment."

"I think that's the second amendment, sir. And you're in a residential development. It is illegal to discharge a firearm in a residential area. Not to mention the illegality of holding a man at gunpoint."

"Ain't you a dandy, with your highfalutin words."

"Sir, we need you to surrender your weapon and let Officer Beanblossom go."

"I'm on my property. I got a right to bear arms. And I got a license. I ain't surrendering nothing. And I'm gonna kill me an officer in about thirty seconds if y'all don't leave me the hell alone."

Johnny glanced at his watch again. He stood to the side of the open front door with just a screen door between him and the subject. Then he heard the roar of a tractor and saw Shaw's head whip around toward the sound. The trooper slipped outside and in two quick steps came up behind Allen Ray Shaw. He put his gun to Shaw's temple and said, "If you don't, I won't."

The old man handed over his weapon. Hank muttered, "Praise be to God" as he rubbed his arm.

Buck came on the front porch as Johnny handcuffed the old man. He looked the trooper straight in the eye and said, "You're hired."

4
APPLE DAY

A faint heart never won a fair lady or stole a watermelon.

~*Jack Wright*

"Darlin', it smells so good in here, I can't keep my nose from twitching." Jack and his Basset hound, Ezmeralda, walked into Tess's kitchen, both with chins raised and noses sniffing the air. Jack stopped in the middle of the kitchen and turned in a full circle, taking in the apple pies that sat on every inch of surface in the room. "I didn't know they were holding the Apple Day Apple Pie Bakeoff right here in your kitchen."

"Oh, don't be silly. You've just entered Tess's test kitchen."

"Woman, just how many pies are you planning on entering?"

"Mister, are you listening? These are just test pies. I want to make sure I'm entering the best kind." She pulled a Dutch apple pie out of the oven, closed the door with her foot, and set the pie on a hot pad near the stove. "I know I'm up against heavy competition."

"If this is a test kitchen, then you are in need of a tes*ter*." Jack smiled broadly. "And I do know a thing or two about apple pies."

"I'll just bet you do." She gave a mock show of looking him over. "Okay, I guess you'll do."

"Man alive, I've never seen so many pies, short of up at Slick & Junebug's. Ezzie, where shall we start?"

"Jack, I love that dog, but you're not feeding my pies to her." Tess shook a pie server at him.

"Oh, she won't eat much," he said absentmindedly, looking over the choices. He leaned toward the pies. "What have we got here?"

"Dutch apple, apple crisp, apple caramel," Tess pointed to each as she named them off, "apple lattice top, apple crumb, upside-down apple pie with walnuts, two crust apple, deep dish apple, and an apple tart."

"Well that one's out right off the bat," he said, pointing to the tart. "It's a pie contest, not a tart contest."

"Just sit yourself down and start eating." Tess pretended to scold him. "I need your taste buds, not your sass."

"It won't matter which one I like best." Jack took a bite of the apple crumb pie. "Because mine's going to be the grand prize winner. Mmmm… dang, this is good."

Tess put her hands on her hips, and she looked incredulous. "*You're* entering a pie in the contest?"

"Why's that so hard to believe? Men can bake too."

"What kind are you entering?"

"I'll let you know once I've sampled all of these," he said, his eyes dancing at her.

THE SUN rose bright and clear the September morning of Apple Day. They had decided Tess should enter her caramel apple pie — a double crust pie with caramel icing on top. Jack said it was so good he couldn't keep his feet still and admitted it might even be a contender against his Dutch apple.

"They said to take the pies to the pie tent. It's over here." Jack led the way through the crowd of people. Main Street was busy with vendors and shoppers filling the street. Barbecue, fried chicken, and fish sandwich booths sat alongside fried apple pie and arts & crafts booths. Big iron vats full of simmering apple butter dotted the street, and men in overalls used six-foot-long wooden paddles to stir the thick deliciousness over an open fire. The air smelled of grease and cinnamon.

"Let's drop off our masterpieces and then go meet up with Louetta at the VFW breakfast feast over at the Methodist church. She wants us to meet her sister."

"Her sister's in town?"

"Yep. Says she's eighty-four going on fifty-four. She came in just for the Apple Day weekend."

Jack and Tess joined the line at the pie tent. There were nineteen ladies, each holding a pie, and they all turned to look at Jack and his pie.

"Are you entering *two* pies, Tess?" Edna Earl looked disapprovingly over the top of her glasses.

"She most certainly is not. What's wrong with y'all? You act like you've never seen a man bake a pie before."

"That's 'cause we haven't." Edna Earl's daughter, Shirleen, examined Jack's pie, looking suspiciously at him. "You mean to tell us *you* made that pie?"

"That's exactly what I mean. And apparently none of y'all have bothered to look at the day's schedule, or you'd know I'm giving the Praise the Lard & Pass the Apple Pie Workshop later this afternoon." Jack's look of satisfaction married the shocked expressions on the women's faces, quieting everyone for a few moments. Finally, Tess found her voice.

"*You . . . you're* giving the cooking class?"

"Does the Pope wear a funny hat?" Jack winked at Tess.

Tess's brow creased. "Aren't you just full of surprises."

"Come on, I'll tell you about it over pancakes."

For three dollars, you got biscuits and gravy, scrambled eggs, cinnamon rolls, pancakes, bacon, apple juice, and coffee at the VFW breakfast. Jack and Tess filled their plates and made their way to Louetta's table.

"Well, there you two are. We were about to send out a search party for you. Y'all, I want you to meet my older sister, Ima Jean." Lou emphasized the words *older sister*. "Imy, this here is Jackson Wright and Tess Tremaine."

"Pleased to meet y'all. You know, she never has introduced me without calling me her *older* sister."

"Well you are my *older* sister. Lawzee, don't be so touchy."

After the plates were empty, Tess leaned in. "Lou, we nearly caused a riot at the pie tent. Did you know Jack's giving the cooking class this afternoon?"

"'Course I did. Didn't you? You two *are* engaged, aren't you?"

"It appears we need to work on communication." Tess shook her head at both of them in mock disgust, but her scowl turned to a bright smile when she saw Martha Maye and Butterbean walking toward them.

"Come on, y'all, they're about to start the Apple Dumpling Pageant."

"Apple Dumpling?" Tess turned to Jack.

"Sure. We have an Apple Day Queen, and an Apple Day Dumpling — kind of like the princess version — it's for little girls four and under."

"Can we walk through the bank lot to see the antique cars on the w —"

"Chester! Over here!" Ima Jean called out, interrupting Louetta and waving to a smarmy-looking man who appeared to be in his sixties. He wore a Hawaiian shirt untucked over baggy, wrinkled khaki pants.

"Who's that, Imy?" Lou put a hand on her sister's shoulder and craned her neck to see the man Ima Jean was enthusiastically waving at.

"That's Chester," Ima Jean said around a tube of lipstick that she was using to paint her lips bright red. Then she popped a peppermint into her mouth.

"Well I gathered that. I'm not deaf. 'Specially since you about busted my eardrum when you called him over here." The women watched Chester as he weaved and bobbed his way through the crowd. "But *who* is he?"

"He's my new suitor. He asked if he could court me, and I graciously accepted."

"Your suitor?" Lou's response came out louder than intended. She lowered her voice. "How did you meet him? How long have you known him? Who are his people?"

"Good green lands, child, you ask too many questions. Now hush. Here he comes."

Chester approached the group with a forced smile and went straight to Ima Jean, planting a wet kiss on her cheek. "I'm sorry I'm so late, sugarplum. Did I miss breakfast?"

Lou looked at Tess and Martha Maye and mouthed, "Sugarplum?"

"We just finished, but I can stay back with you while you eat." She turned to the group. "Y'all go on ahead to the pageant. We'll be along directly."

"Why don't you introduce us to your gentleman friend first, Imy?" Lou's lips pressed together, and her tone suggested she wasn't asking but telling.

"Land sakes, where are my manners? Chester Hale, I'd like you to meet everybody." She went through the introductions and Chester shook hands with Jack and kissed the ladies' hands, including Butterbean, who giggled. When he turned back toward Ima Jean, Lou wiped her hand on the side of her bright red pants, making a face like she wanted to throw up at Tess and Martha Maye.

Ima Jean shooed the group with her hands. "Now y'all g'won, don't let us hold you up, or you're likely to miss the Apple Dumpling Pageant." She waved her fingers in the air.

Lou shot a worried look at her sister but motioned for the group to follow her. "All right, Imy. You join us soon, okay?" Ima Jean waved them on.

Martha Maye saw her mother's furrowed brow and pursed lips. "What's the matter, Mama?"

"You know I have a gift when it comes to reading people. My read on

Chester is something ain't right."

"He seems nice enough to me," Martha Maye said. "I think it's nice Aunt Imy has a beau."

"Yeah, well, unfortunately you didn't inherit my gift for reading people, bless your heart." Lou patted Martha Maye on the back. "Everyone you've ever picked turned out to be — "

"Mama, hush," Martha Maye whispered to her mother. "Lenny's still Butterbean's daddy. Don't talk about him that way in front of her."

"Anyway," Lou continued, "the way Imy's been acting lately, I'm worried about her judgment."

"Mama's afraid Imy has the start of that Old Timer's disease," Martha Maye explained to Jack and Tess.

"What's Old Timer's disease, Mama?" Butterbean tugged on her mother's hand.

"Little pitchers have big ears," Lou said. She turned to her granddaughter. "It means she'd forget her head if it wasn't attached. She's been acting squirrelly lately. Why, she tried to pay the bill twice yesterday at the diner. Good thing Junebug's good people and didn't take advantage of her."

Talk of Ima Jean and her beau were put on hold as the group watched the Apple Dumpling Pageant followed by the Apple Day Parade. Sitting on Jack's wide front porch, watching the Shriner's antics in the parade, Lou's brow was furrowed in worry now; Ima Jean never had rejoined them.

"I wonder whatever happened to them."

"Maybe they went to the Silent Auction."

"Or the Hard Cider Workshop."

"Or the Senior Citizen Craft Fair."

Lou was quiet throughout the rest of the parade. The group hooted and hollered when Pickle passed by in the marching band; they clapped for the politicians, except for Mayor Buck Lyons. They merely politely waved at him, while they oohed and ahhed at the floats.

After the last car in the parade passed by, the group was getting ready to go inside for refreshments when a squad car dashed up the road. Hank pulled into the driveway and stopped with a lurch. He jumped out of his car and hurried to the front porch with a serious expression on his face.

"Officer Beanblossom," Jack said, "what's the matter?"

Hank looked at Lou. "It's Ima Jean, Louetta. She's been taken to the hospital."

5
A Spurious Nature

He's as useless as a blind man's driver's license.

~Louetta Stafford

Martha Maye rushed down the hospital corridor, holding Butterbean's hand and practically pulling her daughter along. She stopped at the end of one hall and looked left and then right. When she saw her mother, Tess, and Jack, she quickly went to them.

"How is she? What on earth happened? " she asked as she rushed up to them.

Lou went to her, wrapping her into a hug. "It was a stroke, honey. It was a pretty bad one, but she's hanging on."

Martha Maye's hand went to her cheek. "Lord have mercy. I can't believe it. She was just with us, fine as day, and now . . . " she looked into the room through the open door, "now she's laying in there hanging on for dear life."

"Don't you worry, hon. Imy's a tough old bird. She's gonna pull through. It — " Lou abruptly stopped talking. Her eyes narrowed at a figure coming toward them.

Chester Hale, looking unconcerned, joined the group. "How is she?"

Stiffly, Louetta said, "She's alive."

Jack took Chester by the arm. "Why don't you come with me, and let's get us a cup a joe?"

"I'm coming too, Jack." Tess turned toward her friend. "Martha Maye, Lou, can I get you all anything?"

"No darlin'. We're just fine." Louetta answered for both of them, shooting a hard look at Chester as he rounded a corner. "We're better now that he's gone. Tell Jack thanks for getting him the heck outta here."

Tess nodded and looked down at Butterbean. "How about you, sweetie?" Butterbean shook her head no, her little face full of worry.

Tess found Jack and Chester in the hospital's small cafe. The men got coffee, and Tess got a Coke. They settled down at a table.

"So, Chester. How long have you known Ima Jean?"

"Aw, about five years, I expect. Long enough to be close friends. I care about what happens to her."

Tess muttered, "More likely you care about what happens to her money."

Jack shot her a look and forged on. "How did you meet?"

"Now there's a funny story. I met her through my friend, Possum."

Jack and Tess gave him a strange look.

"Well, that wasn't his given name, of course. His friends call him Possum. I don't know how he came to be called that. His mama named him Kevin. But I can't call him that. He's Possum to me and always will be Possum to me."

Jack and Tess raised eyebrows.

Chester cleared his throat. "Anyway, he introduced us. At the time, he was sweet on her, and he could tell I took a liking to her myself, but he forbade me to go out with her. Well, he's been my friend for forty-eleven years, and you just don't spit in the face of a friendship that old."

"No. I guess you don't," Jack said over his coffee cup.

"But Possum is in poor health. He doesn't get out much anymore, so Ima Jean and I do. Get out, I mean." He looked from Jack to Tess. "What he don't know won't hurt him. When two people are drawn to each other, you just can't fight the feeling. You know what I mean?"

"So you've been dating Ima Jean without your friend knowing it?"

"Yep. That's about the size of things."

Under his breath, Jack said, "So much for not spitting." He clasped his hands on the table and leaned in, saying in a louder voice, "And just what are your intentions, Mr. Hale?"

"Aw, call me Chester. And I got nothing but good intentions." Chester ignored Jack and turned to Tess. "Don't you worry your pretty little head about that, lil' lady. Ima Jean's good to me, and I'm good to her."

"How so?" Jack cocked an eyebrow.

"You know, I've always wanted to do that." He gestured at Jack's eyebrow. "How do you do it?" His forehead moved up and down and all around, but he couldn't raise one eyebrow without raising the other one too.

"It's a gift." Jack rolled his eyes.

"What sorts of things do you two do — if you don't mind me asking." Tess poured more Coke into her cup.

"Aw, we go out to dinner, and lunch, and . . . " He scratched his head and then chuckled. "I guess those are the main activities. Least the ones I can recount in polite company." He flashed a "you know what I mean" look at Jack. Tess stiffened and blushed.

Jack ignored him. "Who pays for these lunches and dinners?"

"Aw, sometimes I do. Sometimes she does. She's a very generous person."

"I'll bet."

Martha Maye, Butterbean, and Louetta came into the cafeteria just then. Walking up to the table, Lou said, "The doctor said she needs to rest and shouldn't have visitors, so we're going home. You leave her be, Mr. Hale. You hear?" She crossed her arms.

"Yes, ma'am. I was just telling Jack and Tess here what good friends Ima Jean and I've become." He put his hand over his heart. "I do care for her an awful lot."

"And her money," Lou boldly said.

Chester pretended not to hear. "If there's anything I can do, you just call me. I'm staying up at the motel."

"I'll be sure to do that," Lou said stiffly. "I wouldn't wait by the phone if I were you." Lou turned on her heel and marched off.

In the car, as Jack drove everyone home, Martha Maye asked what Lou had against Chester Hale.

"I took an instant dislike to the man. I don't trust him, and I don't like him. And I do trust my sixth sense. It's never wrong."

Martha Maye leaned toward the front seat where her mother sat. "But he hasn't done a thing."

"Doesn't have to. He just exudes a spurious nature."

"What's supurious mean, Granny?"

"Spurious. It means phony. Fake. A charlatan. A pretender." Lou looked out the window and then turned her face back toward Martha Maye. "Imy's been telling me about a man, but I didn't pay it much attention." She twisted in the seat toward the back of the car. "She never named names, but some of the things she told me made me wonder if he wasn't just shining her on."

"Shining her on?" Butterbean's voice went up in question.

Lou nodded. "I think he's been taking advantage of her and her generous nature. She told me she's been giving cash to someone who's down on his luck right now."

Tess spoke up. "He said they go out to eat a lot. Jack asked him who pays, and he said both of them do."

"Maybe I'm old fashioned, but I say a man who lets a woman pay for his meals isn't a man," Lou harrumphed.

6
WELL, BITE MY BUTT AND CALL ME AN APPLE

He's about as crooked as a snake.

~Martha Maye Applewhite

Ima Jean improved over the next few days, while Lou ran herself ragged, dividing her time between hovering over her sister at the hospital and keeping the bookstore open. Tess and Jack decided to do some investigating on their own in Ima Jean's town, forty-five minutes north of Goose Pimple Junction. After moseying around town asking questions, they went to the Butler County Sheriff's Office.

"Chester Hale, Chester Hale . . ." a Detective Galen Rose repeated the name as he searched his computer for any mention of one Chester Hale. Jack and Tess sat on the other side of the desk. "Nothing in the database about him. What's his address?"

"We don't know. Nobody seems to know." Tess raised her hands up helplessly.

"Let me check some other places." His fingers flew over the keyboard, and then he stopped to read. "Do you know of a Betty Ann Holdaway?" The detective looked up from his computer.

Tess sat up straight. "No. Why?"

"Says here they were married once." Galen Rose twirled a pencil between his fingers as he worked.

"Interesting." Jack got up and looked over the detective's shoulder at the computer screen.

The detective looked up. "Have you ever seen him drive a Lexus?"

"We were under the impression he was practically destitute. At least that appears to be the story he's told Ima Jean, and she's told her sister."

"Yeah, and I'll bet he has cancer too."

"Excuse me?" Tess cocked her right ear in his direction.

Galen turned only his face to her. "That's a common line with these con men. They prey on the sympathy of kind people." His eyes went from Tess to his computer screen, which he continued to look at while he talked. "His last known address was 121 Beacher Street. That's what's listed on his driver's license. Says here he owns a 2010 Lexus."

"Oh, my gosh. He really is conning her."

"Looks like. Let me do some investigating, and I'll get back with y'all."

As soon as they left the police station, they drove to 121 Beacher Street. A man in his thirties, who was tossing a ball with a boy in the front yard, said he'd never heard of a Chester Hale. Tess called Lou. She told her what they'd found out so far.

"Well, bite my butt and call me an apple. I've got to warn her. Lessee... it's almost five o'clock. I can't leave the store yet. Pickle's the only other one here. Imy's supposed to come home tomorrow. Do you think it would be all right to wait until then to talk to her? After I leave here, I have to go home and get her room ready. Martha Maye's sitting with her now."

"I don't see what it would hurt," Tess said. "What could he do overnight? Besides, he's a con man, not a murderer. Just do what you have to do. This news will keep until tomorrow."

LOUETTA HELD the cordless phone between her cheek and her shoulder while she wrote down a list of things her sister wanted at the grocery store.

"I'd like some peanuts to snack on and some of that popcorn I can cook."

Lou's forehead scrunched up. "You mean microwave popcorn?"

"Yes. That's it. And I need some peanut butter. I get Jif, and see if you can find some with little bitty peanuts chopped up in it."

"You want chunky peanut butter?"

"Yeah! Chunky. That's what I want. And some cherry jelly — "

Lou interrupted her sister. "You want jam or jelly?"

"Well, whatever. I suppose jam is fruitier. Or preserves. And some thin-sliced white bread too."

"Okay, what else, hon?"

"Some of those Hershey bars. The little bitty ones. A big package of them."

Louetta strained her neck to look out the window for Butterbean. "And you mentioned tissue. Do you still need that?"

"Yes! Thank you. A nose in need needs Puffs indeed."

There was silence for several minutes as Lou didn't know what to say.

Imy resumed, "That should do it. No wait, I need hairspray too. I get that big pink and white can. And go ahead and get me two of those."

"Aqua Net?"

"Yes. That's the one. The humidity is so thick, I've got to have something to hold these curls." Suddenly she sang, "Silk — you go to my head."

Louetta took the phone from her ear and stared at the receiver as if it were a foreign object. Then she put it back to her ear. "All right, honey. I'll run by Food Country, and then I'll be over to the hospital to pick you up and bring you on home. 'K, hon?"

"Food Country's the food specialist," was Ima Jean's answer.

Louetta shook her head and ended the call before her sister came out with any more nonsense.

LOU ARRIVED at eleven o'clock to check out Ima Jean from the hospital and take her home to convalesce. Tess was minding the store, and Martha Maye would join her in the afternoon. It had only been a little over an hour since she talked to her sister. She was worried about her but glad to be taking her home where she could keep an eye on her.

The strange looks on the nurses' faces vaguely registered as Louetta marched past them on the way to Ima Jean's room. "Morning, ladies. Beauty of a day out there."

"Well, yes it is, but--" the nurse said in Lou's wake. "Mizz Stafford . . . "She rounded the counter at the nurses station and went after Lou.

"Mizz Stafford," the nurse repeated as she walked into the hospital room. Lou was standing in the middle of an empty room.

"Where is she?" She turned in a circle as if she would find her sister hiding somewhere in the empty room.

"That's what I was trying to tell you. I thought you knew. She's already gone."

"Gone?" Louetta's face lost all color, and she whirled around to face the nurse.

The nurse quickly amended, "Not *gone*, gone. She's gone home."

"Whatta you mean she's already gone home? I just got here."

"Um . . . yes, ma'am, I see that, but . . . " the nurse bit her lip and twisted a ring on her finger.

"But what? Are you telling me she took a taxi home? I just talked to her a little over an hour ago."

"No ma'am. He said you knew. He said it would be all right. And Ima Jean was happy to go with him, so I didn't see a problem — "

"He? He who? Oh, I just bet I know *he* who — "

"Um . . . " The nurse held up one finger. "I'll be right back."

She came back seconds later with a chart. "It says here Chester Hale was authorized to check Ima Jean out of the hospital."

"Authorized? Who authorized him?" Lou tilted her head and narrowed her eyes.

"Well . . . you." The nurse looked perplexed. "He said he talked to you. And Ima Jean wanted to go with him, so I didn't see a problem . . . "

Lou raced home, mad as a wet hornet that Chester Hale had overstepped his bounds. As she neared her house, she scanned her driveway and the street for any unfamiliar cars but saw none.

Martha Maye and Butterbean were putting the finishing touches on the room Ima Jean would stay in while she convalesced. Lou rushed in, out of breath.

"Mama, where's Aunt Imy? Why are you so out of breath?"

Lou put a hand to her chest as she tried to control her breathing. "You mean she's not here?"

"Of course she's not here. You went to get her." Martha Maye's brow furrowed. "Didn't you?"

Lou told her what happened at the hospital. Martha Maye tried to calm her mother and hazard a guess as to where her aunt could be. "Maybe they stopped for lunch on the way home. You know how much Aunt Imy loves to eat out. After four days of hospital food, she probably just wanted one of Slick's burgers."

An hour later, after Lou had called all the restaurants in town and found out no one had seen Ima Jean today, she started to panic. She called Jack and begged him to take her to Abingdon to check if Chester had taken Ima Jean to his home.

"Jack, I don't think I shoulda waited until today to have that talk with Imy."

Jack pulled out his cell phone. "I'll take you up there, but first I'm calling the law."

7
CHIEF BUTTERFIELD

That's crazier than a dog in a hubcap factory.

~Johnny Butterfield

"Welcome aboard, Chief." Four officers and Bernadette stood in the reception area of the Goose Pimple Junction Police Department, figuratively and literally applauding Johnny's arrival.

"Thank y'all. Thank you very much." He shifted a cardboard moving box from one huge arm to the other and reached out with his other hand to take the ball cap that Skeeter Duke handed him.

"We got you a little welcome to the department gift. It ain't much…" Skeeter shrugged.

Johnny looked at the navy blue hat with white lettering. "GPJPD. Whew, good thing this town doesn't have a longer name. It wouldn't fit on a ball cap. But thank you. I'll wear this with pride." Everyone looked at him expectantly, so he added, "But not in the building."

The men took turns shaking hands with the new chief and clapping him on the back. Bernadette looked at him over her reading glasses. "You refrain from calling me a little lady, and we'll get along just fine."

"I will show you the same respect I do the officers. And if you refrain from telling me what to do, we'll get along just fine." Johnny flashed his lopsided grin, and Bernadette's stern face turned sheepish.

Her ramrod straight posture drooped a little. "Okay, okay, alpha dog established. Can't blame a girl for trying."

Johnny nodded. "It will take some time for us to get to know each other's idiosyncrasies, but I want all y'all to know I'm a straight shooter. I don't tolerate gossip or backstabbing. If you've got something to say, you say it. My motto is plain talk is easily understood. If anyone ever has a problem with me, you come to me first. I want to be the first to hear about it. And I'll afford you the same courtesy." Everyone nodded.

The phone rang, and Bernadette went around the desk to answer it. In a moment, she hung up and turned to Johnny. "Chief, we got us another situation. That was a call from Jackson Wright reporting Lou's sister is missing."

"Missing? Whatta you mean missing?"

"I mean missing. Gone. Absent. Misplaced. Nobody's seen her. Apparently, some ne'er do well told the hospital Louetta gave him authorization to check out Ima Jean. That was the last anybody's seen her."

"Don't that beat all." Johnny slapped his cap against his thigh.

"Yeah. It sure does. Jack and Tess went to Abingdon where Ima Jean lives, but no one has seen hide nor hair of her or Chester." She pushed a pencil through her helmet-like hair. "I just can't believe she's been kidnapped." Bernadette rested her hand over her heart as if to calm its beating.

"Now, now. Nobody said anything about abduction yet."

"What would you call it? She's AWOL. Unaccounted for. Vanished into thin air. And she was last seen with that man."

"Put out a BOLO. Then get me whoever's in charge of law enforcement over in Abingdon."

Bernadette whirled around to get to work. Johnny headed for his new office.

JOHNNY WAS surveying his new office when Bernadette appeared in the doorway. "Chief, that was a weird one."

He turned toward her. "How so?"

"Soon's I got off the horn with the BOLO, old Mr. Hornaday called in." She leaned a hip into the doorjamb and crossed her arms as if she were settling in. "He's over eighty if he's a day. Still driving that big old Cadillac around. His wife passed a few years back. I think he's still got all his faculties, though. Why, I — "

"Bernadette!"

She stopped talking and jerked from leaning to standing.

"Skip the salad and get to the main course."

"Oh." She blushed and shifted from foot to foot. "What I was gonna say is he's old, but he still knows what's what, and he says somebody stopped him over on Tyringham Road."

"And that would be cause to call the police station because . . . " Johnny held out his hand in the air.

"He wanted to know if we had a new police officer."

"News travels fast."

"Around here it travels at the speed of light. But I mean . . . unless you've been stopping citizens and giving out lectures, I don't think he was talking about you."

"Go on."

"We only got six officers on the force, you know, and he says the man who pulled him over ain't one of them. He was calling to complain on account of the guy being a blow-hard. Said he lectured him on the danger of speed, yada yada yada. Mr. Hornaday demanded that the officer be let go. You know – fired, axed, unemployed, out of action." She ran a finger over her throat.

"You're kidding me. Is this some kind of let's-test-the-new-guy sort of thing?"

Her hand went up in the air. "Chief, I kid you not." She crossed her heart with her index finger.

"What did he want?" Johnny slumped into his office chair.

"Who? Mr. Hornaday?"

Johnny took a deep breath and let it out slowly. "No, Bernadette, what did the supposed officer want when he pulled the gentleman over?"

"Oh. Said he was speeding. Didn't give him a ticket or anything, just a lecture and a warning."

"Did he show him a badge?"

"He flashed one right quick, but Hornaday didn't get a good look at it. His eyes ain't what they used to be, you know."

"Tell me he wasn't in a cruiser."

"Nope. He was in an unmarked sedan. No lights up top except for a cherry."

"Anyone can buy one of those. Did he give a description?"

"Nope. Said he didn't think much about it until he got home. Then he got good and mad about the lecture and decided to call it in."

"That is mighty odd. Tell everyone to be on the lookout."

8
CRISIS AVERTED

She's about as bright as a burnt out light bulb in a dark room with no windows.

~Charles Kittedge

Johnny was headed to Louetta's house when Bernadette came over the radio.

"Chief, we got a report of a vehicle stopping at all the mailboxes on Sweetwater. You anywhere nearby and could take a look-see?"

"Roger that, Bernadette." Johnny did a U-turn and headed for the street. As soon as he turned the corner onto Sweetwater Lane, he saw the car and turned on the cruiser's flashing lights. The man's car was pointed in the wrong direction so the driver's side was next to the mailboxes. Johnny pulled up nose-to-nose with the car and got out.

"Z'er a problem, Officer?" The man stuck his long neck out the window.

"Chief. I'm Chief Butterfield and just wondering what it is you're doing." Johnny looked over the top of his sunglasses with the sternest look he had.

The man started stuttering. "W-well, I'm d-delivering the mail, of c-course."

Johnny folded his arms in front of him. "Come again?"

"The mail. I'm a p-postal worker. Charles K-kittedge." The man's Adam's apple bobbed up and down as he extended his hand out the window to shake Johnny's.

Johnny scratched his head and furrowed his brow. "Why are you using a personal vehicle, Mr. Kittedge?"

"The t-truck's in the shop, Chief. I got an identifying t-tag on the back of the car." He hitched his thumb over his shoulder.

Johnny hadn't had a chance to see the back of the man's car since he'd approached him head-on. He walked to the back of the car and saw that, sure enough, the tag identified the car as contracted by the United States Postal Service. Just as he walked back to the driver's window, a woman who looked to be in her mid-seventies came out of her house and walked toward them, pointing her finger at the postal worker.

"That's the man I called about. He's been up and down this street, stopping at every box . . . " She finally saw it was Mr. Kittedge sitting in the car and her face dropped. "Oh, Mr. Kittedge, I didn't mean to call the law on *you*. I had no idea it was you in there. You're always in your mail truck. I, I, I — "

Johnny stepped in and saved her. "No harm done, right, Mr. Kittedge? Better safe than sorry. You did the right thing. Now why don't we let Mr. Kittedge get on with his work? Sorry to have held you up, sir. You have a real good day now."

The woman cupped her hand over her mouth and shouted, "I'm gonna make you a cake, Mr. Kittedge, you hear? I'm awful sorry."

Johnny got back in his cruiser, turned the light off, and called into the station. "Bernadette, you know that strange car stopping at mailboxes on Sweetwater?"

"Yessir."

"It was the postal carrier. Crisis averted."

"Well, if that don't beat all," Bernadette's voice came back.

9
TRYING TIMES CALL FOR FRYING FOOD

"We don't air our dirty laundry out in public."

~Martha Maye Applewhite

"Ima Jean, are you comfortable?" Chester brought a cup of coffee laced with two mg of Xanax into the bedroom and set it on the bedside table next to Ima Jean.

"Need more Calgon!"

Chester gave her a funny look and felt her forehead for fever. "Okay… I'll get some when I go to the store. Right now, you need some coffee." He held up the cup to her lips and tipped it so she could drink. "That's a girl." He set the coffee back on the table and patted the outside of his trouser pockets. "But um . . . I'm a little short right now. Do you think you could loan me a few bucks just to tide me over? I can get some food to cook for you while you're convalescing."

Ima Jean nodded, and he produced her checkbook along with a peppermint. "Look what I brought you, sugarplum." He unwrapped the candy and gave it to Ima Jean.

"Listen, sugar, since I know you're not feeling up to snuff, no need to write out the check. All's you have to do is put your John Henry right there. I'll do the rest." He pointed to the line where she should sign her name. She did so without question.

"Good. Good. Now, I'll be gone for just a bit. When I get back, I'll cook up some supper for my love."

Ima Jean looked at him for a long while. Then she spoke. "I wish I were an Oscar Meyer weiner . . . "

"I do too, sugar." He touched the tip of her nose and followed it up with a kiss. "You've made me very happy by coming here with me, darlin'. I'm going to do everything in my power to make you a happy woman." He picked up the coffee cup. "Here. Drink some more." He made sure she'd drunk all of it before setting it back on the tray. "Now you just rest. Be back in a flash." He patted her arm.

Chester went out to the kitchen and filled out the check for two hundred dollars. He didn't want to raise any eyebrows with a higher number. He wasn't sure how impaired the stroke had made her, but she sure was talking funny. He figured as long as she stayed confused, his plan was good as gold. He smiled to himself at the pun.

"Betty." He wondered where she'd gone off to. "Betty!" he said louder.

A woman with a light dye job, about ten pounds overweight, and in her early sixties, came in through the back door.

"There you are. I've been looking all over for you." He looked her up and down. She was wearing white shorts and a V-neck top that showed a lot of cleavage. "Now let me look at you all over." Instead of looking, he leered.

"Oh, stop," she giggled. Then she saw the car keys in his hand. "You going somewhere?"

"Yep. I'm going to test the waters. If I don't come back within an hour, you get the heck outta Dodge, you hear?"

"Yeah, yeah. We've been over this a million times."

Before he left the house, he made sure Ima Jean was sound asleep. He tapped her forehead and with a wry grin said, "This is your brain. This is your brain on drugs."

MARTHA MAYE brushed her hair with her fingers and straightened her sweater on the way to answer the door. "Johnny. What a nice surprise. Come on in." She stood aside, and Johnny walked in past her, stopping in the hallway.

"I'd like to say this is a social call, but I'm here on official police business." He looked down at her, as he was a good foot taller than she was.

Her eyebrows made a V, and her forehead wrinkled. "Official business?"

"Since I am the acting police chief of Goose Pimple Junction, my first assignment is, sadly, finding your missing aunt. I take it she hasn't surfaced yet?"

Martha Maye shook her head. "Not yet. Come on back to the kitchen, and I'll fix you up with some sweet tea and cookies. Mama, Tess, and Jack should be back soon."

Johnny sat down at the table and noticed a huge bowl full of peppermint candies. "Someone around here like peppermint?" he laughed as he studied the bowl.

"Yeah, Aunt Imy does. She's always got one in her mouth. We bought up a blue million of them just for her. And now she's not here." Martha Maye looked like she was about to cry.

"Don't fret, Martha Maye. I'm gonna find her. Or die trying."

"Oh, I hope not the latter." She had just set down a glass of tea in front of Johnny when they heard voices at the front door. "There they are." Martha Maye hurried to meet them with Johnny close behind. "Didja find her? You did find her, didn't you?"

Lou placed her pocketbook on the hall table and patted her hair into place, shaking her head. Her worried expression changed to one of surprise when she saw Johnny. "Oh! I didn't know you were entertaining, Martha Maye."

"I'm not. I mean — " Martha Maye twisted a ring on her finger and shifted from foot to foot.

Johnny swallowed a bite of cookie, still holding a good portion of it. "She means I'm here on account of Ima Jean." He watched Lou, as her eyes went from the cookie in his hand back to his face. "She's being hospitable." He held up the cookie. "We're allowed to eat on duty."

"'Course she is and 'course you are. Where are my manners? Jack, Tess, can I get y'all anything?"

Jack gave Tess a one-armed hug and kissed her cheek, keeping his hand around her waist. "I've got all the sweetness I need, Louetta." He looked at his watch. "I'm gonna feed Ezmerelda right quick. She gets cranky if her supper's late."

"Speaking of eating, come on y'all. Trying times call for frying food." Lou led the way back to the kitchen. She wrapped a big white apron with red flowers around her waist and pulled out her iron skillet, Crisco, and chicken thighs and legs. While she began preparing the chicken for frying, she asked why they'd called in a state trooper to find her sister.

Johnny filled everybody in on his new position as police chief, and Jack related what they'd found out about Chester.

"So you don't believe this is an act of love? That he took her somewhere because he loves her?" Johnny asked.

"If that was his reason, why'd he lie about having my permission, and why hasn't he or she called to tell us she's all right?" Martha Maye slapped her hand down on the table. "No, sir. That man is nothing but a waste of skin."

"I knew that ten-gallon mouth was full of hot air. All that talk about how much he *cared* for Ima Jean." Lou scrunched her mouth into a scowl. "Then right under our noses, he swooped in and stole Imy. And I stood by like a bump on a log and let it happen."

"Lou, it's all my fault, don't blame yourself." Tess flopped into a chair at the kitchen table. "I'm the one who told you to wait until today to warn her about that charlatan."

"Don't you start talking like that, Tessie. I've been making my own decisions since I was knee-high to nothing. If anything happens to her, it's all my fault."

"It's nobody's fault but the abductor's, and when I'm done with him, he's gonna be standing in the need of prayer." Johnny pulled out a notebook and pen from his shirt pocket. "Now. Y'all tell me all y'all know about one Mr. Chester Hale."

"He's been cashing her checks. I know that for a fact."

"How do you know that?"

"I called up Ima Jean's bank and pretended to be her." She talked as she battered the chicken. "I know all her information, see. So I asked them to give me her balance—'cept I said *my* – and they gave it to me. Then I asked what were the last checks to clear, and lo and behold, Mr. Chester Hale has cashed a bunch, totaling $2,500."

Lou put the chicken pieces into the hot oil, and it sizzled and popped. She washed and dried her hands, salt and peppered the chicken, and joined everyone at the table.

"Johnny, have another cookie." Martha Maye shoved the plate at him.

"Do you think she wrote the checks on her own accord?" He took a cookie from the plate, nodded thanks to Martha Maye, and returned his attention to Lou.

"No I don't, Chief. The teller told me the signatures were different handwriting than the rest of the checks."

Around a bite of cookie, Johnny said, "I'll put an alert out to all the banks in town to be on the lookout for any checks signed by Ima Jean Moxley. And I'll get them to fax me the images of the checks." He scribbled some notes and looked up at Louetta. "Have you thought of anywhere he might have taken her? Even a long shot is worth looking into."

Lou huffed. "I'm assuming he took her back to his lair." She wrung her hands. "I just don't know."

Johnny reached for her hand and gave it a squeeze. "We're getting closer, Lou. I should be able to find out his address." He winked at her and then flipped his notebook closed, placing it back in his pocket. "Okay, y'all hang tough, and I'll get to work." He put his hands on his knees, pushing up to stand. "We've already put a BOLO out for Chester. We'll find him. Don't you worry."

"I know you will, Johnny. I mean Chief." Lou stood with him. "Well, we don't want to keep you."

He laughed and looked at Martha Maye. "Oh, you can keep me." But he stood and grabbed two more cookies on his way out.

As they reached the door, Lou said, "You're welcome here anytime for dinner or cookies. That's an open invitation."

"I'll remember that, Lou. Thank you." He held up a cookie. "These are delicious." Stepping outside, he said, "I'll keep you informed of any developments. "I'll be at the police station until we catch this yahoo. I'll catnap on the cot in the back."

"Well, don't you eat nothing to spoil your appetite. Just as soon as this chicken is done, Martha Maye will run some over to you."

Suddenly the cookie he'd been holding in his hand was no longer there. He looked down to see a Basset hound chewing and looking at him forlornly with big bloodshot eyes.

"Ezzie! Ezzie, come here." Jack came across the yard, scolding his dog. "I saw that. You owe the chief an apology. Man alive, I opened the door to let her out and she made a beeline for that cookie."

She wagged her tail and licked her lips. Martha Maye disappeared inside the house.

"I'm so sorry, Johnny. She's a Houdini and a thief. You gotta watch her." Jack scooped her up in his arms.

"I didn't even know she was there. She's a stealthy little thing." Johnny reached out to pet her head.

"Yeah, and she's not going to be little much longer if she keeps eating cookies."

Martha Maye came back out with a baggie full of cookies. She looked sternly at Ezzie, who looked hopefully back at her. "Uh-uh. These are for the chief, you little cookie monster."

"I'm going to head to the station right now." He looked at his watch. "I still have time to alert the banks. I'll keep y'all posted." He looked at

Ezzie and pointed. "And you, you little thief. Don't make me take you to the pokey for petty larceny."

Ezzie had the nerve to bark at him.

10
TALK OF THE TOWN

He may be good-looking, but good-looking won't put food on the table.

~Willa Jean Coomer

Downtown Goose Pimple Junction was bustling the next morning when Johnny parked his car and walked a block to the diner. The yellow tickets that were stuck under windshield wipers on some of the cars vaguely registered with him because Ima Jean's abduction was on his mind, and he didn't have room to think of much else. Periodically, he thought about Martha Maye and how pretty she looked when she'd brought him fried chicken, home fries, macaroni salad, and a slice of apple pie. But he forced his mind back to Ima Jean and how he was going to go about finding her.

The diner was crowded but went deadly silent when he walked in. Everyone stopped talking, and all heads turned his way. He met a few people's eyes, nodded a hello, mumbled "Morning," and sat down at the counter next to a man who looked older than Moses.

"You're mighty brave to bring yourself in here today, Chief. I myself don't hold no ill will, but then again, I ain't got a car, so it's no skin off my nose."

"Come again—" Johnny started to say, but Willa Jean interrupted him.

"What can I getcha, *Chief?*" She put an emphasis on "Chief" but the word was dripping with disdain.

Johnny wondered if it was his imagination or was she glaring slightly at him? He put a hand to the back of his neck as he craned his head around, finding several other people giving him the same expression. *Curious.*

"Coffee, a fried egg, and cheese grits, please." He flashed her his best grin, but she didn't seem to notice.

She turned on her heel without another word, calling to Slick, "A deadeye and mystery in the alley, Slick."

Johnny noticed the old man cackling to himself and wondered what was so funny. He seemed to be a regular. Surely he was used to diner lingo. Moses turned to the man next to him and mumbled something that sounded like, "I haven't had this much fun since the pigs ate my brother."

Willa Jean came back with a cup and saucer and a pot of coffee. As she poured the brown liquid into the cup, a good amount spilled into the saucer. She looked up at Johnny and deadpanned, "Oops," but she walked away, making no attempt to clean it up.

Conversation had started again in the diner, but it was in hushed tones, not the loud chatter that Johnny had heard when he first came in. Once again, he looked around the restaurant and noticed furtive glances coming at him. A few words and bits of sentences wafted his way: "a lot of gall, arrogant, outsider, amateur, dumb as a fencepost . . . " He considered asking the gentleman next to him if this was normal townsfolk behavior, but Willa Jean came back and set a plate in front of him. His gaze went from the plate to her eyes, which seemed to hold a challenge.

"Um . . . ma'am . . . this looks right tasty, but it also looks like *poached* eggs and *hash*."

Willa put all her weight on her right leg and propped her hand on her hip. "Least your eyes work."

"Well, see . . . I could be mistaken, but I thought I ordered fried eggs and grits."

"You're mistaken." She flung a towel over her shoulder and walked away.

Johnny looked at Moses and said, "I'm late to the party. Wanna tell me what's going on?"

"Oooh, law," the man drawled. "That was almost as ugly as Uncle Moody's divorce." He swiveled off his stool, saying, "'Scuse me. I have to see a man about a horse," and he made his way to the restrooms.

JOHNNY CAME in the back door of the police department and immediately detected a problem. Raised, angry voices came from the front reception area. He followed the racket and found the room full of an angry mob, facing down a cowed Bernadette and Officers Beanblossom and Duke. He briefly wondered if the department had riot gear.

Putting two fingers in his mouth, he whistled loudly and then held up his hands in the air. Some folks stopped talking, but he had to say, "Now, now, folks, simmer down" before the room got completely quiet. "Someone wanna tell me what in the world is going on?"

Choruses of "I'll tell you what's going on" rang out from the crowd, and he held up his hands again.

"Bernadette, you first."

"Well, Chief," she began.

"*Acting* Chief," someone corrected.

"Chief," she said again, shooting a look at the rude person, "these here folks are riled up on account of getting parking tickets that carry a fine of $100."

Everyone in the crowd held up yellow tickets, accompanied by shouts of "In all my born days," and "This is a travesty."

The front door opened and the crowd parted to let Caledonia Culpepper through. She was dressed in a bright pink sundress and had pearls around her neck. She too held a yellow ticket and walked right up to Johnny.

"Not you too," Johnny groaned.

"Chief, it's lovely to see you again." The crowd grunted and sent out objections, but she was undeterred. "I wondered if I might have a moment of your time." She flashed a brilliant smile.

"Well, Ms. Culpepper, I'm kinda busy at the moment — "

"Caledonia."

"Caledonia. I'm kind of in the middle of something — "

"I can see that, Chief. But I believe I have something that might clear all this up. Just a moment of your time," she repeated.

His gaze leveled on her, but he finally relented. "Officers, keep the peace out here while I have a word with Ms. — um . . . Caledonia. Folks, form a line, please, and Bernadette will issue receipts one at a time as you pay your fine."

Renewed choruses of "I'm not paying one red dime," and "Don't unpack your things," rang out, as he ushered Caledonia to his office.

"And I was told this was a friendly town." He sank into the chair behind the empty desk.

"It is. But there's something funny going on. You see, I had a parking ticket a while ago — " She sat down and crossed her long legs.

"Yes, I remember you were on your way to pay it when I ran into you and Martha Maye. The first one didn't deter you from parking illegally again?"

She gave him another hundred-watt smile. "See, here's the thing. This ticket is different than the first one." She handed him a yellow ticket. "When I first looked at it, I thought it was some kind of a joke. I even tossed it into the waste can in my car because I was so sure it wasn't real."

"What made you think that?"

She handed him the ticket. "They're not the same."

He studied the ticket and was immediately surprised to see his name signed as the ticketing officer. "That isn't my signature."

"I was over to the school when I heard about half the town being ticketed. I hightailed it right over, and from the looks of things, I didn't get here a moment too soon."

Johnny read over the ticket and then called for Officer Beanblossom, who appeared in the doorway within seconds.

"Officer, do you have a parking ticket on you?"

Hank reached into his back pocket and pulled out some yellow tickets that resembled the one in Johnny's hand.

"See, Chief? Someone's playing a practical joke on either you or the town." She held out Hank's ticket. "See how this one has 'Goose Pimple Junction Police Department' at the top, and this one," she pointed to the fake ticket, "it doesn't have anything but 'Parking Violation' on it. This one," she pointed back at Hank's ticket, "has a number at the top, it asks for a lot more information on the offending car, and it lists the potential offenses. This one," back to the fake, "just has a paragraph of mumbo jumbo stating the fine and what will happen if it's not paid in seven days."

"It's easy to procure fake tickets online, Chief," Hank offered.

"Who would do this?" Johnny asked, sitting back in his chair, slightly slump-shouldered.

"Nobody on the force, Chief. I can guarantee you that."

Johnny swiped his hand over his face, took a deep breath, squared his shoulders, and went to tell the angry mob that they were not going to be paying any fines today.

11
DONUT WHISPERER

I've been to two goat ropings and a county fair, and I ain't seen nothing like this.

~*Pickle Culpepper*

Word spread fast about the bogus tickets. Johnny sent his officers out to collect as many as they could and to stop into the businesses in town to relate the situation to folks in case gossip took a wrong turn.

"The only thing that spreads faster than small-town gossip is kudzu," Johnny said, "and sometimes it's a wash."

The police department was finally getting back to normal when a call came in about Chester Hale.

"Chief, this here's Officer Hurley over in Butler County. I think I got a bead on your BOLO."

"Yeah?"

"Affirmative. I spotted somebody fitting the description coming out of the Piggly Wiggly. I've detained him, pending your instructions."

"Good work, Officer. I'll send one of my men to pick him up momentarily. Sit tight."

"Will do, Chief."

Johnny had just dispatched Officers Northington and Woodson to pick up the suspect when Bernadette appeared at his door. Johnny raised his eyebrows, waiting for what she would say.

"Chief, it's another Culpepper here to see you." She blew a bubble with her gum.

"Another one?" Johnny cocked his head.

She pulled the bubble back into her mouth. "Yessir. It's Pickle this time."

"Well, send the boy back." Johnny got up and walked to the office door. Pickle appeared moments later with a worried look on his face and a T-shirt that said: DONUT WHISPERER.

"Pickle, I hope you're not in any trouble, son." Johnny offered his hand to the teenager.

"Uh . . . no sir. But I think you might be." Pickle's Adam's apple bobbed.

Johnny motioned for Pickle to have a seat, and as both of them sat in chairs on either side of the desk, the chief said, "Oh?"

"Well, first of all, I might as well tell you." Pickle puffed out his cheeks. "I was speeding."

Johnny merely raised his eyebrows and waited for the boy to continue.

Pickle scooted to the edge of his seat. "See, I was driving over on George Cannon Road when an unmarked car with a light up top came up behind me." He scratched his nose. "I pulled over to the side of the road, and this man I've never seen got out and came up to my window. Said I was speeding and he was gonna have to write me a ticket. I was suspicious right off, 'cause like I said, I never seen him before. I asked to see his badge, and he flashed me one."

"Were you able to get a good look at it?" Johnny rested his arms on the desk and leaned toward Pickle.

"Yessir. It was a gold badge with an eagle at the top. The word 'Chief' was right under that and 'Goose Pimple Junction' was right under that. A blue circle thingy was under that in the middle of the badge with a picture of something . . . I'm not sure what . . . I didn't get a good enough look before he put it away."

"You say it had the word 'Chief' on it?"

"Yessir. And I knew that wasn't right. But I didn't say anything."

"Smart boy."

"Yessir. So he started writing me out a ticket, and while he went around to the back of my car to take down my license plate number, I pulled up the picture app on my phone."

Johnny momentarily went slack-jawed. "You're not as dumb as you look." He held out a hand. "No offense."

"Yessir. None taken. I get that a lot." He offered a weak smile. "Anyhoo, I put my phone on mute and snapped a picture." He took out his phone and pulled up the picture, giving the phone to Johnny. "And here it is. There's a good bit of distance and the back windshield between us, and it's pretty dirty, but it's something, right?"

"Quick thinking and excellent work, Pickle. I'm real proud of you."

Pickle blushed. "It's not that big a deal." He looked at his shoes.

"It certainly is. Thanks to you, we now have a picture . . . of sorts . . . of this perp, which is bound to help us apprehend him a whole lot faster. Good work, son."

Johnny emailed the picture on Pickle's phone to himself, then printed it out, and gave it to Bernadette to copy, distribute, and post online.

As he walked Pickle to the door with his hand on the boy's shoulder, he said, "I meant what I said. You should give law enforcement some serious thought."

"Yessir."

Nodding to the teenager's T-shirt, Johnny stage-whispered, "Looks like you already have the right diet."

WHEN PICKLE walked into the bookstore to report for work, Martha Maye held out her arm. "Step back, Jack."

Pickle looked to his left and right and then behind him. "Ma'am? It's me, Pickle, not Jack."

Martha Maye's scowl turned to a smile. "I know, darlin'. But I do not want to see or hear about anything having to do with donuts. Honey Winchester's offered to be my personal slave driver, I mean trainer, and she made me swear off anything that tastes good."

"Well, I can't change my name, but I can go and change shirts if you want." Pickle scratched his head.

"No, Pickle." Martha Maye laughed. "I'm just funning you. I'm going to have to learn something called willpower. Even if it kills me trying."

He nodded but still looked confused. Tess saved him.

"What's Honey got you doing, Martha Maye?"

"Oh, Lord. She's drawn up an exercise plan that calls for *activities* I can do at home, and which are nothing short of torture, plus something called jogging. I told her I'd start at walking real fast and see how it goes from there."

"I can tell you're losing weight already."

"Really?" Her face lit up. "Oh, I hope so. I'd hate to think all this misery is for nothing."

"So . . . have you seen Johnny lately?" Tess smiled widely.

Martha Maye blushed and smiled back. "Yes. His first assignment as chief is to find Aunt Imy." She looked over her shoulder to make sure nobody was listening. "I'd never seen him out of his trooper uniform before, except for the other day when he had on a suit for the interview." Martha Maye leaned toward Tess. "Which he filled out quite nicely, I might add." She giggled. "Now that he's chief, he wears regular clothes and that cute baseball cap with *GPJPD Chief* on it." She closed her eyes and shook her head. "My, that man knows how to wear a pair of jeans."

"Martha Maye, you tickle me." Tess gave her a one-arm hug.

"I know, I know, you think I'm a fool to be thinking about another man, so soon after the . . . " she searched for a word, " . . . wretched misfortune with he-who-is-dead-to-me." She sighed heavily. "My taste in men is sorely wanting. And I know I must come across as unfeeling, seeing how Aunt Imy's missing and all. But a girl can dream."

"I know you're worried sick about your aunt, just as all of us are. But worrying isn't going to find her. I think it's good you have something to take your mind off the situation. Johnny seems like a catch, Martha Maye. Just go slow, and you'll be all right."

"The only thing slow about me is my metabolism. But I'll try. Just yank a knot in my head if you see me going all man crazy. Okay?"

Tess smiled at her friend and squeezed her arm. "Will do, Martha Maye. Will do."

The bell at the front door tinkled, and Hank Beanblossom came in.

"Officer Beanblossom, it's a pleasure to see you. Doing some shopping today?" Tess asked.

He pulled a folded piece of paper from his front pocket. "Naw, just here to pass the news and show y'all a picture of a suspect we want to talk to." He handed the picture to Tess, and Martha Maye scrunched in close to look too. "He's passing himself off as the chief and writing all kinds of bogus tickets. We thought folks were going to gather pitchforks and storm town hall there for a while. Then we figured it out — thanks to the Culpeppers — " he glanced and nodded to Pickle "— that the man's an impostor. We don't have a name on him yet. Just want y'all to help spread the word and keep your eye out for him."

"Land's sakes," Martha Maye shook her head, "he doesn't look like a criminal. What's wrong with people anyhow?"

"Don't rightly know, Martha Maye. It takes all kinds, doesn't it?"

Officers Northington and Woodson walked the suspect into the police station and took him immediately to Johnny's office.

"Good afternoon, Mr. Hale." As Chester sat in the chair in front of the desk, Johnny came around the front of it and propped a hip on the corner, looking down at the man.

"Mind telling me why I'm here?" Chester's scowl didn't deter Johnny.

"You're here because you checked Ima Jean Moxley out of the hospital, and not only that, you did it on a pretty tall tale."

Chester sat stone-faced, so Johnny continued.

"She hasn't been seen since, which makes you the last person to have seen her before she disappeared. I'm liking you pretty good for a count of kidnapping, sir."

This time Johnny waited out Chester's silence.

Finally, Chester spoke. "I only did what Ima Jean asked me to do. She said her busybody sister would smother her with care. She begged me to take her out of there."

Johnny unwrapped a stick of gum and stuck it in his mouth, all the while staring at Chester. "Is that right?"

"It most certainly is." Chester sat up straight, jutted his chin, and puffed out his chest.

"Then you won't mind taking me to her and letting me check out your little story."

"I most certainly do mind. I won't break her confidence. She wants to convalesce in peace and quiet, and that's exactly what I'm going to give her."

"Are you her lawyer?"

Chester shrugged. "No. I am not."

"Are you her doctor?"

Chester frowned. "No."

"Then I don't see a problem breaking a *confidence* in the name of allowing the law to be certain of Ms. Moxley's well-being. We'll talk to her, and if everything is as you say it is, we'll leave her be."

"I'm sorry, Chief. I won't do it." He folded his arms and looked as if he were pouting.

Johnny stood up and reached for the handcuffs on his belt. "Then I'm afraid you're under arrest for kidnapping and impeding an investigation."

"Now hold on just a galldern minute." Chester held his hands out. "Maybe we can work something out."

"Yeah? Like what?" Johnny loomed over him.

"Suppose I call Ms. Moxley and let you talk to her? She can assure you of her safety and happiness, and I can be on my way."

Johnny looked doubtful, but acquiesced. "I suppose that's a start." He watched as Chester took out his cell phone and punched in some numbers.

"Ima Jean, it's me, Chester. Yeah, yeah, I know. I got waylaid a bit. Listen, I'm over to the Goose Pimple Junction Police Station. Yes, you heard me right. They snatched me up and forced me to come over here. They're accusing me of kidnapping you. No, I'm not kidding. Chief Butterfield would like to talk to you and hear for hisself that you're safe and sound. Mmm hmmm. Okay. I'll put him on."

Johnny took the phone from Chester, taking note of the number on the screen. "Ms. Moxley? Yes, this is Chief Butterfield. How are you feeling, ma'am?" The voice on the other end of the phone was weak but sure. Johnny listened for a bit. "I'm glad to hear that, ma'am. Can you tell me where you are?" Johnny kept his eyes on Chester as he listened.

"Yes, I expect you are in a bed, but do you know whose house you're in?" Johnny stood up and went around to his desk. He took a pen and began scribbling notes.

"Mizz Moxley, I apologize for waking you from a sound sleep — " Johnny held the phone from his ear, and a raised voice spilled out.

"Yes, ma'am. But your sister is mighty worried. Yes, ma'am, I do know that milk does a body good."

Chester coughed into his hand to try to hide a smile, but Johnny saw it.

"Yes, but 'you're soaking in it' doesn't tell me where you are, ma'am. It just tells me you like Palmolive dish soap. It would be extremely helpful, ma'am, if you could tell me your whereab — " Johnny pinched his nose, momentarily closing his eyes against the frustration of the round and round conversation.

"We'll confirm and then leave you be. Yes, ma'am. But I'm afraid I —" Johnny stopped talking. There was no use in continuing. There was no longer anyone on the other end of the line. Johnny held the phone in the air. "She hung up."

"I done told you she didn't want to be disturbed. Maybe now you'll believe me." Chester snatched back the phone.

"She didn't exactly sound all right to me. She sounded very confused and a little dotty."

"Yeah, she sounds that way, but believe me, she's right as rain."

"I'm afraid I still need to verify with my own two eyes. Why don't I drive you home now, Mr. Hale." Johnny hadn't said it as a question, but Chester took it as one.

"No, thank you, Chief. I'll call for a ride back. Tomorrow, if Ms. Moxley is still speaking to me, I'll bring her to the station for you to *see with your own two eyes*." His tone was mocking.

Johnny would have liked to slap the smirk off the man's face. Instead, he insisted the man bring in Ima Jean today, bid him good day, and stepped out into the hall, pulling with him Northington and Woodson, who had been standing in the doorway during the interview.

Watching Chester walk down the hallway, he told the men in a low voice, "I want y'all to follow him. Don't let him see you, but don't let him out of your sight. I'm afraid he won't go to her if he knows we're following him. I'll get Judge Woosley over in Butler County to sign a warrant to search the house. Only problem is, I don't know if he's got her at his place or somewhere else, so once y'all see where he goes, call it in. When I talk to the sheriff over there to alert them that you might need assistance, I'll ask if one of their men can bring the warrant to you. Y'all just keep your eyes on the suspect."

"Yessir, Chief. We're on it." The officers hurried down the hall and out the back door to get their car in place for the tail.

12
CHESTER PULLED A FAST ONE

A lie doesn't care who tells it. It will jump out of anybody's mouth.

~Chester Hale

Johnny pushed away from his computer ten minutes after Chester left his office. It appeared that the number Chester had dialed was a throwaway. He swiped his hand over his face and stood. He went down the hall and around the corner and told Bernadette he was going out for a bit. Then he drove to Louetta's house.

Martha Maye came to the door in shorts and a T-shirt, wiping sweat from her red face.

"Did I catch you at a bad time?"

"Heavens no. You saved me. Now I can take a break. Honey Winchester's going to drive me to drink with the exercise regime she's got me on." Johnny took off his cap as he entered the house, trying hard not to stare at Martha Maye's legs. Now his face was the red one when he saw Louetta rushing toward him, her ample hips moving up and down as she walked.

"Did you find her? Tell me you found her." The worried expression on her face nearly broke his heart.

He took her by the elbow and led her to a chair. She listened intently while he related the events of the day. He finished up with, "But I feel pretty confident that she's all right, Lou. She didn't sound distressed, just a bit confused. She even got a little mad at me for disturbing her nap. She didn't sound like a woman in an adverse situation."

Martha Maye put her arm around her mother's shoulders.

"What exactly did she say, Johnny? Tell me word for word." Lou absentmindedly patted her daughter's hand.

Johnny related the conversation to her.

She shook her head defiantly. "Then that couldn't have been my sister. She would never in a million years talk to anyone, let alone a chief of police, in such a manner. And I know for a fact she would never hang up on anybody. She's far too well-bred for that kind of behavior."

"Well, she did just have a stroke."

"Nope. Not a million years, would she, Martha Maye?"

Martha Maye shook her head. "I can't see her acting the fool like that."

Johnny puffed out his cheeks and thought a minute. "Tell me, Lou, I never spoke with your sister. Does she have sort of a nasally voice?"

Louetta looked like she'd just been poked with a hot iron. "Heavens no. Imy has a soft, gentle voice. The voice of a southern lady."

Johnny closed his eyes and looked at the ceiling. "I'd be willing to bet that old Chester Hale pulled a fast one over on me." He hung his head. "I should have known. Dadblast it, I blew it."

GRAVEL POPPED under the cruiser as it pulled out behind a gold Chrysler convertible, driven by a woman, with Chester as a passenger. Northington kept a respectable distance but had to increase his speed to keep the convertible in view. "She's flying like a bat outta hell," Woodson said.

They drove out of downtown Goose Pimple Junction and followed the car onto the freeway. The car exceeded the speed limit, but Hank stayed six cars back. They were discussing whether they should pull her over for speeding when they entered the next county.

"Too late now." Northington banged the steering wheel with his hand. "We lost jurisdiction. We woulda blown our cover anyway."

"Yeah, but we'd have the woman's name." Woodson craned his neck to see around a pickup truck directly in front of them. "No matter. I have the license plate number. We'll find out who she is. But keep following and we may do one better than that."

When Northington didn't answer, Woodson added, "We may find Ms. Moxley."

"Well duh. Nothing gets lost on you, does it?"

"Aw, hush up," Woodson grumbled.

The road had narrowed from a four-lane divided highway to a two-lane road. The pickup truck in front of the officers slowed to make a left turn, and a tractor-trailer a little farther up pulled onto the road into the cruiser's lane.

"Hold up." Woodson rolled his window down and pulled himself halfway out of the car so he could see past the tractor-trailer. He pushed back inside the car and just about bounced out of his seat. "She's braking. The brake lights are coming on. Get up there, fast!"

"What do you think I'm trying to do? I can't get around this tractor." They were driving about 20 mph with Woodson on the edge of his seat. He kept squirming and bouncing, as if it would help move the vehicle faster. They turned onto the next road, and finally, they saw a flash of gold.

"There they are!" They entered a neighborhood with ranch-style houses built in the '60s. After the woman and Chester turned into one of the driveways, Northington pulled over a few houses away and reached for the radio.

"Base to unit six. You there, Bernie?"

"I'm here, Vic."

"We're at 1811 Walker Street."

"10-4, Vic." She came back in a few seconds. "I show that house belongs to one Betty Ann Holdaway. The chief says hold your position. A unit from Butler County will meet you there directly."

"Roger that."

13
1-800-CASH-NOW

When you do a job, be proud enough to put your name on it.

~Officer Northington

Northington, Woodson, and Beanblossom stood on the front porch, and Woodson rang the bell. A woman who looked to be in her sixties opened the door. She had bleached-blonde teased hair, a skirt too short for a woman of that age, and a blouse that had too many buttons undone. She was chewing gum like a cow chewing cud.

"Yeah?" was her greeting.

"Ma'am, we have a warrant to search the premises. May we come in?"

"What for?"

"It's all here in the warrant." Northington pushed past the woman, and the two officers followed him inside the house.

They walked past Chester in the hallway. With a smug look on his face, he said, "You're wasting your time. She ain't here, boys."

Northington barked, "Woodson, you take the basement; Beanblossom, you take the attic. I'll check the bedrooms."

When they'd searched the house and had seen no sign of Ima Jean, they met back in the living room where they suddenly realized Betty Ann and Chester were no longer in the house.

Hank Beanblossom's phone rang the very instant Northington said, "I'll be a son of a biscuit," and Woodson ran out the front door.

Hank got off the phone as Woodson was coming back inside the house. "That was the chief. He says he got hornswoggled. Said the woman he talked to on the phone back at the house wasn't no Ima Jean Moxley."

Woodson shook his head. "Well, he's not the only one to get

hornswoggled today. They done skipped out on us. The car's clean gone."

CHESTER WAS sitting at Ima Jean's bedside when she awoke. Her eyes darted around the room. "Where am I?"

"Why you're convalescing with me, pumpkin. Looka here," he picked up a bowl of applesauce, "try some of this." He spooned some into her mouth.

"Less filling. Tastes great." She smacked her lips.

"Imy, you're a kook, you know that?" He helped her sit up slightly and then placed a tray with a turkey TV dinner and a bowl of applesauce on top of her lap.

"Tinkle," she said.

He helped her up, but she stopped when she saw a woman standing in the room.

"Who're you?"

"This is your nurse, hon. This is . . . um . . . "

The woman cut in. "I'm Betty. Here, let me help you to the bathroom."

When she stepped back into the room, Chester said, "See? I told you that script I gave you was accurate."

"You were right. She's a kook. But why'd I have to say all that? Why couldn't I justa sounded confused?"

"'Cause her sister heard her talking that commercial talk in the hospital. We gotta keep up the pretense."

"She's getting more steady on her feet. That worries me."

"Well, Nurse Betty will just up her happy pills." Betty checked on Ima Jean and helped her back to bed.

Chester turned on the TV and changed the channel to *Wheel of Fortune*, which they watched while she ate. When she was finished, he asked if she'd like some ice cream, but she declined. That was fine with him. He'd put the dose of Xanax in the applesauce. She wouldn't be awake much longer.

He shot a look at Betty before addressing Ima Jean. "Say, beautiful, we're in need of some more cash so's I can take proper care of you."

"Call 1-800-CASH-NOW." She didn't take her eyes off the TV show, so he turned her face to look at him.

"You funnin' me?" He looked suspiciously into her eyes, but she swatted his hand away and resumed watching the show.

Taking out her checkbook and a pen from his back pocket, he said, "Just put your John Hancock right here, sugar," he cooed, pointing to the signature line, "and we'll be good to go."

She signed her name quickly, so he thought he'd press his luck.

"And sign one more just in case. Then I'll reward you with your favorite candy." He shoved another check in front of her and unwrapped a peppermint candy while she signed her name.

"In case what?"

"Say! You can talk other than in commercials." *Not for long*, he thought. *You'll be off in dreamland soon.* Chester looked around and then at the TV and shouted, "Buy a vowel, you fool." It worked. Ima Jean forgot all about what they were saying. He waited until the show was over and had another idea.

"Ima Jean, would you do me a big favor, hon?"

"What's that?"

"Would you sign your name right here?" He put another check down in front of her and handed her the pen. "And right here. There you go. Okay, how about a few more? This is good practice to get your fine motor skills back up, isn't it?"

She shrugged and continued to sign her name. After the sixth one, she put the pen down and laid her head back on the pillow. "I'm tired."

"You did real good, sugar. Now you just rest. Stay right here, and I'll be back in a jiffy."

"Choosy mother's choose Jif," she said with her eyes closed and head still on the pillow.

"Yes, they sure do, sugar." He took the tray away and went to the kitchen. Betty followed.

Slumping into a chair and propping his elbows on the table, he said, "If only I knew her PIN, I wouldn't have to worry about the bank tellers. But she didn't know what I was talking about when I asked her."

"No matter. Your bright idea will produce the same results." Betty plopped into a kitchen chair. "But either one of us is gonna have trouble showing our faces out in public, don't you know. I'm sure they've got one of them BOGOs out on us."

He looked at her as if corn were growing from her ears. "BOGO? Don't you know it's BOLO? Be On The Lookout, *not* Buy One Get One free. Sheesh. Women." Chester rubbed his chin, thinking. Then he pounded his palm against his forehead. "I shoulda thought of this before now." He stood up, excited, and headed for the basement door.

"Thought of what?" Betty asked, following him.

"I need to convince them she's not here with me so I'll have time to cash these checks."

"How're you gonna do that?" They stepped into the dark, dank basement. Cobwebs hung down here and there. It smelled musty and felt creepy. Betty crossed her arms in front of her but followed Chester. He led her to a wall of bricks.

"This here is the answer to our problems." He patted the wall.

"A brick wall?" She shot him a look that said he was dumb as a fence post.

"Not just a brick wall." He began removing bricks until he had taken out enough for Betty to look inside.

"I'll be darned. It's a room." She leaned in and looked carefully at the secret room.

"It sure is. When I bought this old place, I had some remodeling done, see. One day one of the workers called me up, and it was obvious he pretty nearly was shaking like a leaf. I could hear it in his voice. He said he thought they'd found a room down in the basement, but nobody wanted to look on account of what they might find. Well, I talked him into looking. Nobody and nothing was in it, but I later found out that it was prolly used in the underground railroad."

Betty looked confused.

"See, there's prolly a tunnel that runs right up to this brick wall. They'd have people crawl through, and they'd take down this brick wall to get them in there. Then they'd brick it back up without mortar to hide them in the room while the authorities searched the house."

"It can't be more than seven or eight feet long. Maybe four feet wide." Betty was still looking through the hole Chester had made.

"Just big enough to hide someone. Which is exactly what we're gonna do."

Wide-eyed, she clapped him on the back. "You're a genius."

"Go out and buy me a cot. Here. Take Imy's credit card. She won't mind." He gave her the card as his face morphed into a Grinch-like grin. "But go a couple counties over just to be safe. And if you get pulled over, just say I forced you to leave your house and then gave you the slip."

After Betty returned with the cot and they got it set up with blankets and a pillow, she turned to Chester. "Let's go out and celebrate." She looked at her watch. "It's almost ten-thirty. We can sneak up to Check's for a bit. Lord knows, this town rolls up the sidewalks at ten."

Chester nodded and led the way up the steps. He went to check on Ima Jean. Sure enough, she was lying with her mouth slightly open, softly snoring. He clicked off the TV and watched to see if she awoke. She didn't, so they closed the door and headed for Check's bar.

Sitting at the bar instead of a table, he ordered a Colt 45 and Betty ordered a screwdriver. He looked over each shoulder. The bartender brought their drinks.

"There's been some folks in here looking for you." He wiped off the countertop as he spoke.

"Oh, yeah? Who? And what did you tell them?"

"GPJ police. Told 'em I ain't never laid eyes on you." He nodded toward the beer bottle. "That bottle will cost you extra tonight."

"Okay, okay." Chester laid a fifty-dollar bill on the bar. "That about cover it?"

The bartender shrugged. "For now."

"I'm glad I ran into you." Chester took a pull from the beer. "You know of any lawyer types 'round here? You know what I'm looking for. Someone discreet."

"Think I do." He rubbed a spot out of a glass. "There's a lady comes in here every now and again."

"I'd be obliged if you'd introduce me." Chester brought the bottle almost to his lips and looked the bartender in the eye. The man nodded and walked away.

It was forty-five minutes later that a dowdy woman wearing glasses and a Dutch-boy hairstyle sat down next to Chester at the bar. "You looking for an attorney at law?"

Chester leaned back and looked the woman up and down. He figured her for mid-sixties. She wore a seersucker blazer, periwinkle blue pants with an elastic waistband, and Hush Puppy shoes. He nodded and said, "Matter of fact, I am." He stuck his hand out. "Chester Hale."

"Delores D. Petty. Folks call me D. D." They shook hands and she added, "And who might this be?" She nodded toward Betty, and Chester introduced them.

"What can I do for y'all?"

"Well, Ms. Petty, I need someone to draw up some power of attorney papers and file them for me."

"Do I want to know the details?"

"I doubt it." Chester signaled the bartender for another beer. "What're you having?"

D.D. told the man a bourbon, straight up, then turned to Chester. "My fee will be $2,500 plus traveling expenses."

Chester nodded, thinking he'd just get Ima Jean to sign another check for the lawyer.

"When and where?"

Chester gave the woman the address, and they decided to meet tomorrow at 10 a.m. He gave the attorney a few more details to put in the document and answered her questions. Downing the last of the bottle, he held up a finger to the bartender. "I believe I'll have a bourbon now, my good man. Since I'm about to be a man of means, I might as well start acting like one."

D.D. looked at Chester out of the corner of her eyes. "I'm not going to be sorry I got involved in this, am I?"

"I'm assuming this isn't the first shady deal you've ever done." The slight didn't register a reaction from the attorney, so Chester continued. "Even if someone questions it, the woman trusts me completely and remembers hardly anything. It'll be a piece of cake."

14
BE PREPARED

That lawyer's ugly as a wart hog and half as smart.

~Chester Hale

The next morning, Chester let Ms. Petty into the house and asked to see the document before he led her back to the bedroom. He'd just given Ima Jean another dose of Xanax, this time hiding it in some instant pudding. She was still licking the chocolate off her lips when they walked in.

"Ima Jean, this here's Delores D. Petty."

She tried to sit up, saying, "Who?"

Ms. Petty walked up to her and took her hand. "Please call me D.D."

Ima Jean looked questioningly at Chester.

"Delores D. here's whatchacall a counselor. She came for a visit, peanut."

Ima Jean looked annoyed.

"I've had an idea," Chester said, pulling a pen out of his pocket.

"Ford's got a better idea." Ima Jean frowned.

Chester and D.D. looked at each other and then at Ima Jean. "What?" she said grumpily, crinkling her brow.

"I got to thinking about you and your health, and frankly, sugar, it's got me worried sick. What if something happened and you couldn't give the doctors permission to treat you? You've had one stroke. God forbid you have another, but I think we should be prepared."

The lawyer produced the power of attorney document, putting it on the tray in front of Ima Jean.

Chester pointed to the line at the bottom. "Sign your name right here, pumpkin."

She looked suspiciously at him. "What is this? It looks official to me. What am I signing?"

"Well, to tell you the truth, you're signing power of attorney papers."

"What for?" She tried to sit up straighter, but Chester put a hand on her shoulder and she settled back down to a reclining position.

"Just as a precaution. You've been so sick, I just want to make sure you're taken care of in your time of need. It's mostly for health care. I'll be able to say yay or nay to any procedures they might need to perform. You do trust me, don'tcha?"

"Louetta ought to be my power of attorney. She's kin."

He leaned toward her and took her hand. "Yes, but do you see Louetta anywhere around in your time of need?"

"Well . . . no."

"So . . . see? My motto is be prepared." He gave her a dazzling smile.

"I thought that was the Boy Scouts' motto." Ima Jean took the pen that Chester thrust at her.

Chester mumbled, "I thought it was the villain's in *Lion King*" while at the same time pointing to the line at the bottom of the document. "Right here, sugar britches."

"You're too good to me, Chester."

"I'd do anything for you." He tried his best to look sincere. He glanced at the attorney, who pursed her lips and pushed her glasses up over her ugly black eyes.

WHILE CHESTER was arranging Ima Jean in her new "room," Betty got in her car and drove around until a cop recognized the car and plates and pulled her over. Johnny got the call mid-morning.

"What you want us to do with her, Chief? Far's I can tell, she ain't broke any laws."

"She impersonated the victim. But I know, I know . . . we can't prove that just yet. Tell her she's wanted for some questioning. I'm on my way there. Get her to take you to Chester and then question both of them. He's got to have her. He's going to too much trouble to throw us off."

"Will do, Chief. I'll keep you posted."

Johnny told Bernadette where he was going and went out to his personal car, a blue Ford Taurus, and got in.

REPORTS OF an officer stopping cars and giving out warnings had continued. The *Goose Pimple Gazette* ran an article alerting people to the imposter's hoax, and the town buzzed with talk of it, yet, when stopped, most folks were too scared to do anything but listen to the stern lecture and then report it to the police when they got home. The imposter was always gone by the time real GPJ officers got to the area where the latest offense had occurred. A few brave souls gave him a real talking to, but that just made the man more aggressive, and they always backed down. Clearly the charlatan was crazy enough to be impersonating a police officer; nobody wanted to escalate his craziness.

Johnny was zipping down Clyde Bird Road on the way to find Ima Jean when he saw a familiar person up ahead, and the sights got considerably better. She was alternating jogging and walking, and he slowed the car so that he could watch her for a bit. When he started feeling like a stalker, he sped up and drove alongside her.

"Morning, Martha Maye." He silently chided himself for not being able to think of anything more clever to say.

She slowed to a walking pace and puffed out, "Good morning to you, Chief. Any news on Aunt Imy?"

His car crept alongside of her. "Possibly. Local police called. They've apprehended Chester's accomplice. I'm heading over there now."

"Then you should get on. I know that man's got her. You gotta go find her."

Johnny looked out the front windshield at the tree-lined, sun-dappled road. It was beautiful out here. And in his view, Martha Maye was even more beautiful. For the life of him, he couldn't think of a thing more to say. And he did need to find Ima Jean. He turned back to her. "All right. I got criminals to catch, and I expect you want to get on with your run."

She let out a short burst of air, suggesting his statement was ridiculous. "Walk is more like it. But yeah, these pounds won't disappear with me just moseying." She patted her thighs.

"You look awful good to me." It just popped out. He hadn't planned on saying that, but his tongue was faster than his brain. He hoped his sunglasses hid his mortification.

She blushed and said, "Thank you. It's not true, but I appreciate you saying it."

Johnny accelerated the car and then let up a bit and leaned out the window, looking back at Martha Maye. "It is too true!" Then he sped off, smiling.

15
THE BADGE

He's so stupid, mind readers charge him half price.

~*Johnny Butterfield*

Johnny stepped on the accelerator. He was singing along with Garth Brooks to "American Honky-Tonk Bar Association" when he looked in his rear view mirror and saw a car with a red light flashing on top. He whistled and said aloud, "Well, well, well. Would you looka here."

Pulling over to the side of the road, he turned the Taurus off and waited. His windows were already down on account of the beautiful weather. He took off his GPJPD cap and sat it upside down on the passenger seat. A man in a police uniform walked up to him, but it wasn't one of his officers. He could tell right away that the man had attitude oozing from every pore of his body. *This is gonna be fun.* He smiled and looked up at the man.

"Sir, are you aware you were speeding?"

Johnny kept a straight face. "No, sir, I'm not. How fast was I going?"

"You were driving fifty-seven in a forty-five. Can I see your license and registration, please?"

"Well, Officer, I sure am sorry. I didn't realize I was going that fast. Garth and I were just lost in song, I guess."

The man bent down to look in the passenger seat. Seeing it empty, he looked questioningly at Johnny.

"Garth Brooks," Johnny explained.

The man looked blankly at Johnny.

"On CD." Johnny smiled, but one was not returned.

He reached for his registration and then turned back toward the man.

"You know, I don't believe I know you. What did you say your name was?"

"I didn't."

"Well, why not?"

"Why not what?"

"Why haven't you told me your name? Is it a secret?"

"Sir, don't get cute with me. I'll do the questioning if you don't mind. License and registration."

"It's just that—"

The man interrupted him. "Sir, do not try my patience. You've been pulled over for exceeding the speed limit. That is a careless and reckless violation. I ought to take you into the station, but since it's the first time I've stopped you, I'm gonna let you off with a ticket and a promise to mind the law from now on. This isn't something to be taken lightly, sir. You're old enough to know better."

"You know my age?" Johnny looked incredulous.

The man looked put out. He took a deep breath and said through his teeth, "I might, if you'd produce your license."

"Oh, yeah, yeah, yeah." He leaned toward the glove compartment again and then straightened back up to address the impostor. "How long you worked for the GPJPD?"

"Sir. I'm not going to ask again. License. And. Registration." He enunciated each word slowly, expressing his displeasure.

"Okay, okay. You don't have to get all huffy. Most folks around here are friendly. Who put a burr in your saddle today?"

"Sir. Step out of the car."

"Why? I'm getting the registration just like you asked. I'm just saying—"

"*Sir.* Step out, please. *Now.*"

Johnny peered up at him, trying to look intimidated. "What're you going to do to me?"

The man reached for the handle and opened the car door. "Out." He hitched a thumb over his shoulder.

"Okay, okay. Geez." Johnny stepped out, holding his hands in the air. Pointing to the man's car, he said, "Why aren't you driving a cruiser?"

"It's in the shop. Now if you'll stop with your lame-brained questions—"

Johnny interrupted. "I just got one more question."

The man let out a deep sigh. "What is it?"

"Do you have a badge?"

The man reached into his pocket and flashed a badge, then put it back before Johnny had barely had a chance to look at it.

"That's not a badge," Johnny said, shaking his head and pointing to where the man had just put it.

The man puffed out his chest even though Johnny was taller and bigger than he was. "It most certainly is, and I'm of good mind to arrest you."

"Naw, naw. That there's not a badge." He reached into his back pocket and produced his police badge, holding it up in front of the man. "This here's a badge."

The look on the man's face was priceless. It changed from annoyance to confusion to realization to terror in five seconds.

Johnny crossed his arms over his chest. "I'll bet you got some fake parking tickets to go along with that fake badge."

The man turned and started to run to his car. Johnny made two long strides while simultaneously pulling out his handcuffs from the back of his belt. He caught the man by one arm, flung him down on the hood of the car, and handcuffed and frisked him.

"You ought to be ashamed of yourself. You have the right to remain silent," Johnny began.

16
NOT AN OUNCE OF MORAL FIBER

When she puts on her lipstick, it keeps backing down the tube.

~Chester Hale

The arrest of the impostor put Johnny behind. He had to laugh to himself when he thought of the man's excuse for the ruse: "I'd rather have a sister actively serving in a whore house than have some lame-brain for a chief of police."

Everybody's entitled to his opinion but not to break the law, Johnny thought.

He'd been informed by phone that the woman accomplice had taken the local police to Chester's house, and they had searched it thoroughly with Chester's blessing.

"That still isn't proof he doesn't have her somewhere."

"Yeah, well, there still isn't proof that he does. We keep on him without a valid reason, he's going to cry harassment."

"No, he's not. He wants to be as far under the radar as possible. If you ask me, this was set up."

"What do you mean, set up?"

"I mean, he has her, and he stashed her somewhere else."

"Well, when you figure out that somewhere else, you let me know."

Johnny needed some time to think. He passed a bar, did a U-turn, and pulled into the mostly empty parking lot.

Once inside, he thought Check's looked like General Robert E. Lee might have been a patron at one time. Still, it was a good place for him to sit and ponder. He found a stool at the bar.

"Help ya?" the bartender said.

"Blue Moon if you have it."

"We do. Coming right up." When the bartender returned, he eyed Johnny for several moments. "Don't think I've seen you in here before."

"That's probably because I haven't been in here before." He gave a good-natured grin to the man.

"What brings you in now? Just passing through town?"

Johnny reached for the picture in his pocket. "No, I'm here on police business. I'm looking for a woman, and I think this man," he said as he slid the picture of Chester to the bartender, "might have something to do with her disappearance." Johnny was good at reading people, and he saw the slight arch of the man's eyebrows when he first saw Chester's face. "Do you know him?"

The man shook his head. "Naw, can't rightly say that I do." He wouldn't meet Johnny's gaze.

"How much did he pay you?"

"Come again?"

Johnny took a long pull from the bottle while studying the man. "I think you do know him, and I think he probably paid you for your silence."

"Mister, I don't like your innuendoes – "

"Oh, well, you misunderstood me then. I'm not innuendoing anything. I've got an elderly sick woman out there somewhere, and I aim to find her. I think you can help because I think this man's been in here." Johnny's index finger landed hard on the photo of Chester lying on the bar. "Now you can either level with me, or I can call the Health Department and get them over here." Johnny gave two crisp nods that strengthened his claim.

"Okay, okay, don't get your cows running. Sheesh." The bartender wiped his forehead with a towel from under the bar. Then he leaned in close to Johnny. "He was in here last night. Said he was looking for a lawyer, and I got the feeling he wanted one who . . ." He paused, searching for the right word. "Let's just say I called someone for him who I happen to know doesn't possess an ounce of moral fiber."

"I see." Johnny ran the bottle through his hands several times. "And just what set this one apart from other lawyers?"

The bartender laughed politely. "Good one."

"Did you hear any part of their conversation?"

"Might have."

Johnny got out his money clip and laid a hundred on the bar.

The man pocketed it in one smooth move. "I might have heard them using words like 'power' and 'attorney.'"

Johnny's eyebrows shot to his hairline. "No joke?"

He crossed his arms and leveled his gaze at Johnny. "I kid you not."

"Huh." Johnny stared off into space. "I'm gonna need the name of that shyster lawyer."

"I'm gonna need more than a hundred."

Johnny looked over his shoulder at the pool table in the corner of the room. "Tell you what. You and I play a game of pool, and we play double or everything."

"Huh?"

"Double, meaning if you win, I give you another hundred. Everything, meaning if I win, you tell me everything, *and* give me the hundred back."

A man who'd been drinking Miller Light and sitting at the other end of the bar listening to the conversation finally spoke up. "G'won, Glenn. You can take him. You play at least once a day. Go for it, man."

Glenn pointed his thumb at Johnny. "He must be pretty confident if he's offering a deal like that." He sized Johnny up for several moments. "Tell you what. There's nobody in here now, so I'll take that bet, but in a game of Cricket."

Johnny frowned, and Glenn hitched his head at the dartboard in the back of the room. "Darts. The winner 'closes out' numbers 15-20 three times."

Miller Light spoke up again. "Thatta boy. That's even better. You're great at darts. Hell, you're damn near a dart whisperer. And take a look at him. He's got hands the size of coconuts. Ain't no darts gonna fit in his hands the right way."

"Okay." Johnny stood. "You're on."

They each took a practice throw, and Glenn got closest to the double bull, so he got to throw first to start the game. He stood leaning forward, which offered less stability. His dart landed in the yellow area under the 4. Johnny stood upright, with his right foot in front and left foot in back, and smoothly launched the dart straight forward. His dart landed in the black double bull under the 18. He walked over to the chalkboard and put two marks to the left of the 18.

The game proceeded, and Glenn wasn't bad at darts, but Johnny was better. He only launched a few duds, and he hit the green bull twice and the red bull once. When he added the last mark next to number 20, he tallied up all the points. Johnny won by 25.

His grin wasn't cocky or proud but just plain confident. "I'll be needing my hundred back and the name of that shyster lawyer if you please."

"MONEY-GRUBBING, EVIL-HEARTED, low-down, good-for-nothing attorney." Johnny was at Jack's house, complaining about the stall in the hunt for Ima Jean. "She's lower than a mole's belly button on digging day. She's lower than — "

"Whoa, whoa, whoa! Hold up there. What's got you so riled up?"

"She knows where Ima Jean is, but she won't help me because she's 'bound by attorney-client privilege.'" Johnny mimicked a soprano voice.

"Well, she has a point — "

"I'd be willing to lay odds on her getting Ima Jean to sign power of attorney papers. What else would you need a lawyer for? And Chester supposedly needed a lawyer."

Jack sat up on the edge of the sofa. He looked left then right.

"What's the matter?"

"Ezmerelda. She's too quiet. Usually she's in here pestering you to death to rub her ears, but she's nowhere to be seen." He stood up and headed for the doorway leading to the hall. "Ezzie!"

The Basset hound came slinking in, looking guilty as sin. Her head was down, but her big, bloodshot eyes looked up at Jack.

"What have you been up to?" He put his hands on his hips and glared at the dog. She sat down and hung her head. "What's that on your face?" Jack pulled some shredded lettuce off the side of Ezzie's mouth.

"Aha! The first bit of evidence. What have you been eating?"

Johnny joined them and said, "Uh, Jack, it's probably my fault. I had a sandwich in my backpack, and I set it on the foyer floor when I came in."

"And that big schnozz sniffed it out, did it?" He looked at the dog accusingly. Shame was written all over her face. Her eyes moved up to Jack's, then down, then up again. She was too ashamed to hold his gaze.

"That dog is something else."

"She's something else, all right. I have a good mind to — "

"No, really, Jack. She's got some serious olfactory skills there. Maybe we could use her to find Ima Jean."

"Come again? You want to use this sack of hair with a nose in the line of duty?" Jack snickered. "Are you gonna deputize her?"

"Jack, I'm serious. They said that Ima Jean loves peppermint candy and eats it all the time. I'll bet if we let Ezzie eat some peppermints, she'll want more. She could go into that house and sniff out Ima Jean. And she's gotta be there. Unless he killed her and buried her body somewhere."

"Johnny! Cut that out!"

"Sorry. I'm just trying to be realistic. The real world doesn't always have a happy ending like in the movies."

"Well, okay, but I think we should do a little training with her to make sure she's up to the task."

"Totally doable."

As they both expected, Ezzie was a natural. They let her eat the peppermint candy and then hid some in a room. Her nose led her right to it every time.

"I feel good about this, Jack. If he has her like I suspect, Ezzie's going to find her for us."

Jack crossed his arms. "What if Ima Jean doesn't have any peppermints?"

"That would be like saying what if the sky didn't have the sun. Martha Maye said she's addicted to the things."

Jack looked at his dog. "Ezmerelda, you've got a big nose and a big job. Don't let us down."

17
WORKING LIKE A DOG

That man is flat out rude. He don't have any home training.

~Ima Jean Moxley

Through his window, Chester watched the police chief and another man get out of a car in his driveway. *Why's that local yokel back here?*

The police chief opened the back car door and a Basset hound jumped out, landing on her stumpy little legs. She ate something from the chief's hand and then they all headed for the front door. Chester waited until the bell rang to go to the door. He didn't want it to appear that he'd been watching them.

"Chief, I done told you I don't know where Ms. Moxley is."

"Yessir. I know that. I just wondered if we could come in and ask you a few more questions."

"The mutt too?" Chester pointed at Ezzie, who looked solemnly back at him.

Jack spoke up. "She's a full-bred Basset hound, not a mutt. And she has impeccable manners."

"It's too hot to leave her in the car, and we didn't plan on stopping anywhere, so we didn't think to bring a leash. We promise she won't disrupt your household."

Chester stood aside, and they filed through the door.

Ezzie trotted inside like she owned the place, and her nose led the way. Once in the kitchen, she sniffed all the low-lying cabinets until Jack scolded her. Then she shot out of the room like her tail was on fire.

"Where's she going? I don't like dogs in my house, you know."

"She's just checking out all the new smells in here. She'll be fine. Now, tell us, Chester, what did you say your relationship was with Ms. Moxley?"

But Chester was too nervous about having the dog loose in his house, and he followed after Ezzie. Soon, the three men and one dog were in the bedroom where Ima Jean had been convalescing up until a day ago. Ezzie's nose covered every inch of the carpet, and she sprang onto the wastepaper basket, knocking it on its side. Burrowing her nose into the contents, she came out with a mouthful of peppermint wrappers. She lay down on the ground with the paper between her paws and began chewing it.

"If you wouldn't mind, could you get your dadblamed dog out of here? Look at the mess she made." Chester quickly scooped up the wastebasket contents and the candy wrappers from Ezzie, then shooed everyone out. "If you can't control that dog, I'm gonna have to ask all y'all to leave."

"She didn't mean any harm. Ezzie's just naturally curious, aren't you, girl?" Back in the kitchen, Jack bent down to pet his dog on her head. He whispered something to her and again put his closed hand up to her nose. The dog sniffed, then sneezed, chomped on something hard, and then turned around in a circle, barking and looking up at her owner.

Jack stood, and Ezzie led him to the basement door. Before Chester could get there, Jack opened it, saying, "What's in here?"

Ezzie shot down the stairs, and Chester's heart plummeted to his stomach.

"I'm asking nicely one more time: y'all need to leave. If you don't, I'm calling the law." He was shouting this as he followed the two men who were following Ezzie down the steps. "There's nothing down here but cobwebs and spiders." Chester reached the bottom of the stairs and stood frozen as he watched Ezzie sniffing crazily around the edge of the room where Ima Jean was being held. He smacked his hands together and rushed toward her, when all of a sudden, a voice came from inside the wall.

"I've fallen, and I can't get up."

Chester stopped in his tracks. Then he started yelling, hoping to drown out Ima Jean. But it was too late.

"What was that?" Johnny said, moving toward the brick wall.

"That must've been Betty from upstairs. I'll bet she just got here. Let's g'won up and see."

Ezzie's toenails made tapping sounds as she danced up and down the wall, trying to figure out how to get inside. Jack and Johnny ran their hands up and down it.

"What was that?" Johnny shouted at the wall.

The voice came again: "When E.F. Hutton talks, people listen."

"Ms. Moxley, is that you?" Johnny put his ear to the wall.

"You've come a long way, baby," the voice said.

Johnny whirled around on Chester, who was starting up the steps. "Oh, no, you don't. You get back down here and tell us how to get her outta there." He caught the man at the collar on the back of his shirt, tugging on it. "Get her out before I smack the fire outta you." Chester stared at him, and Johnny added, "Now."

Chester muttered something about police brutality and then hung his head, appearing like a dead man walking as he headed for the wall. "I can explain . . . "

"I'd like to hear you try, you low-down, lying, dirty cur dog. If brains were lard, you'd be hard pressed to grease a pan."

Jack chimed in. "I think a half-wit gave him a piece of his mind, and he held onto it."

Chester began dismantling the bricks, and Johnny and Jack helped once they saw what he was doing. Ezzie was going so berserk, Jack picked her up and placed her in the room once they'd gotten half the bricks down. She rushed to Ima Jean and then sat next to her and barked. When Jack looked up, she looked back as if to say, "Piece of cake."

"We're going to take you back to your sister, Ms. Moxley. Hold on one more minute, and we'll get you out of this place," Johnny spoke soothingly to her.

Her answer was: "How do you spell relief? R-O-L-A-I-D-S."

On the way home, Ima Jean sat in the back passenger seat. At every stop sign, she'd say, "Pots." She did this four or five times and then she wondered out loud, "Just where are these pots and how much are they selling them for?"

Johnny looked at Jack, who whispered, "Well, old Chester was right about one thing: she ain't right in the head."

THE END

RECIPES

Apple Upside-Down Pie

You will need:
apple pie filling
crust
pie topping
salted caramel sauce

Salted Caramel Sauce
2 cups granulated sugar
1½ sticks unsalted butter (¾ cup)
1 cup heavy whipping cream
1 tablespoon (or more or less) sea salt

In a thick-bottomed, heavy saucepan, cook the sugar on low-medium heat.
Do not stir the sugar, but you can swirl the pan around to mix it that way.
The sugar will begin to turn an amber color.
Watch the sugar carefully as it can burn quite easily. Once it reaches 350°,
add all of the butter, whisking quickly to combine.
Remove the saucepan from the heat and whisk in heavy cream.
Mix in salt and let cool.
Once cool, pour into an airtight container.

Prepare the crust:
2 cups flour
½ teaspoon salt
6 tablespoons shortening
2 tablespoons cold butter
7 tablespoons orange juice

In a large bowl mix together the flour and salt and then cut in the shortening
and butter. Once the mixture resembles crumbs, slowly add the orange
juice. With a fork, mix until the mixture begins to form a ball. Divide ball
into two pieces, wrap in plastic wrap, and refrigerate at least 30 minutes.

Pie Topping:
4 tablespoons butter, melted
½ cup brown sugar
½ cup pecans or walnuts

Preheat oven to 375° and line a 9-inch deep-dish pie plate with foil and HEAVILY grease with cooking spray.

Combine butter, brown sugar, and pecans.

Place mixture evenly on bottom of pie plate.

Make apple filling:

6 to 8 tart apples, peeled, cored and thinly sliced

¾ to 1 cup sugar

2 tablespoons flour

½ teaspoon cinnamon

2 tablespoons butter

Mix together the apples, flour, sugar, and salt.

Roll one ball of pastry out to fit the pie plate.

Place half of apple mixture evenly on bottom of pastry; drizzle ¼ cup salted caramel on top, place remaining apples, then another ¼ cup salted caramel.

Roll out second ball of pastry to fit the pie.

Place on top and seal both pastry pieces together, you do not need to make a beautiful design because the pie is going to be flipped upside down.

Make sure to still cut four 1-inch slits in the piecrust before baking.

Bake for 50-55 minutes. Check pie after 35 minutes. If crust is becoming too brown, cover with foil for remaining baking time.

Let pie cool on wire rack for 15 minutes.

Place serving dish on top of the pie and flip over.

Drizzle pie with remaining salted caramel.

Serve with ice cream or whipped cream.

Dutch Apple Pie

Apple Filling
6 to 8 tart apples, peeled, cored and thinly sliced
¾ to 1 cup sugar
2 tablespoons flour
½ teaspoon cinnamon
2 tablespoons butter
Pastry for a 9-inch pie

Preheat oven to 350°.
Make pie shells; put one shell in a pie plate. Crimp edges.
Combine the apples, sugar, flour, and cinnamon. Mix well.
Pour the apple mixture into the pie shell in the plate.
Dot top with butter.

Crumb mixture:
¾ cup flour
¼ cup granulated sugar
¼ cup brown sugar, packed
⅓ cup butter

Mix all ingredients until coarsely crumbled.
Top the apple mixture with the crumb mixture to use on top of the pie instead of a top piecrust.
Bake at 350° for 45 minutes to 1 hour.

CARAMEL APPLE PIE

You will need:
2 9-inch piecrusts
apple pie filling (from Dutch Apple recipe)
caramel icing

Prepare the two piecrusts. Put one crust in a 9-inch pie plate; roll out the second crust. Let it sit between wax paper while you prepare the apple filling.

Apple filling
6 to 8 tart apples, peeled, cored and thinly sliced
¾ to 1 cup sugar
2 tablespoons flour
½ to 1 teaspoon cinnamon
2 tablespoons butter

Combine the apples, sugar, flour, and cinnamon; mix well.
Pour mixture into the piecrust in the pie plate.
Dot with the top of the apple mixture with the butter.
Place the second piecrust on top of the apple filling.
Crimp the bottom crust's edges with the top crust.
Poke a few holes in the top for air.
Bake at 350° 45 minutes to 1 hour or until crust is browned.
While the pie is cooling, make the caramel icing.

Caramel icing
2 cups brown sugar
dash salt
1 tablespoon light corn syrup
1 tablespoon butter
¾ cup milk
1 teaspoon vanilla
1 cup pecans or walnuts (optional)

Combine the sugar, salt, corn syrup, butter and milk.
Cook, stirring until the sugar dissolves, to softball stage.

Cool at room temperature without stirring, until the mixture is lukewarm (110°).

Add the vanilla.

Beat until the mixture holds its shape.

Add nuts if using. Mix well.

Quickly spread the frosting over the top piecrust.

Allow to completely cool before serving.

Once the pie is cool and the icing is ready, pour it over the top piecrust. Let sit for an hour to set up.

Acknowledgements

I'd like to thank the readers who messaged me asking, "How did Tess and Jack get married?" and "How did Johnny become police chief?" and "When are you going to write another book?" Your interest, encouragement, support, and kind words about Goose Pimple Junction are what keep me going. Thank you!

Thank you to my father, John Spears, for the stories he's told me all my life; to Lisa Binion for her fine editing; and to Ellen Mansoor Collier for reading and re-reading this manuscript! I also thank Emily Tippets and E.M. Tippets Book Designs for formatting this book and Anne Rackley for capturing the essence of Ezzie for the front cover image.

And once again, thank you to my family for letting me spend so much time in Goose Pimple Junction.

ABOUT THE AUTHOR

Amy Metz is the author of the Goose Pimple Junction mystery series. She is a former first grade teacher and the mother of two sons. When not actively engaged in writing, enjoying her family, or surfing Facebook or Pinterest, Amy can usually be found with a mixing spoon, camera, or book in one hand and a glass of sweet tea in the other. Amy lives in Louisville, Kentucky.

Please look for book 1 in the series, *Murder & Mayhem in Goose Pimple Junction*, and book 2, *Heroes & Hooligans in Goose Pimple Junction,* available in paperback and ebook. And visit Amy at amymetz.com.

www.ingramcontent.com/pod-product-compliance
Lightning Source LLC
Chambersburg PA
CBHW031834170626
46807CB00004B/1462